MY LiFe
as
Crocodile Junk Food

BOOKS BY BILL MYERS

Children's Series
McGee and Me! (12 books)

The Incredible Worlds of Wally McDoogle:
—*My Life As a Smashed Burrito with Extra Hot Sauce*
—*My Life As Alien Monster Bait*
—*My Life As a Broken Bungee Cord*
—*My Life As Crocodile Junk Food*
—*My Life As Dinosaur Dental Floss*
—*My Life As a Torpedo Test Target*
—*My Life As a Human Hockey Puck*
—*My Life As an Afterthought Astronaut*
—*My Life As Reindeer Road Kill*
—*My Life As a Toasted Time Traveler*
—*My Life As Polluted Pond Scum*

Fantasy Series
Journeys to Fayrah:
—*The Portal*
—*The Experiment*
—*The Whirlwind*
—*The Tablet*

Teen Series
Forbidden Doors:
—*The Society*
—*The Deceived*
—*The Spell*
—*The Haunting*
—*The Guardian*
—*The Encounter*

Adult Books
Christ B.C.
Blood of Heaven

the incredible worlds of **Wally McDoogle**

MY LiFe
as
Crocodile Junk Food

B I L L   M Y E R S

WORD PUBLISHING
Dallas·London·Vancouver·Melbourne

MY LIFE AS CROCODILE JUNK FOOD

Unless otherwise indicated, Scripture quotations are from
the *International Children's Bible, New Century Version*,
copyright © 1983, 1986, 1988 by Word Publishing.

Scripture quotations marked (NIV) are from The New
International Version of the Bible, copyright © 1978 by
the New York International Bible Society.

Library of Congress Cataloging-in-Publication Data

Myers, Bill, 1953–
    My life as crocodile junk food / Bill Myers.
       p.   cm. — (The Incredible worlds of Wally McDoogle ; #4)

    Summary: Twelve-year-old Wally visits missionaries in the
South American rain forest, and stumbles into a series of what
he thinks are impossible predicaments, until he understands
the commandment to put others first.
    ISBN 0–8499–3405–2
    [1. Missionaries—Fiction. 2. Christian life—Fiction.
3. Humorous stories.] I. Title. II. Series: Myers, Bill, 1953–
The incredible worlds of Wally McDoogle ; #4.
PZ7.M98234Mys   1993
[Fic]—dc20   92-46748
                                            CIP
                                            AC

Printed in the United States of America

7 8 9 QPB 11

To Mackenzie—
Thank you for your joy, laughter, and love.

"He [Jesus] said to them, 'There are a great many people to harvest. But there are only a few workers to harvest them. God owns the harvest. Pray to God that he will send more workers to help gather his harvest.'"

—Luke 10:2

Contents

Chapter 1

Just for Starters . . .

"WHAT ARE YOU DOING?" I shouted over the roar of the airplane engines.

The pilot threw our plane into a steep turn. By *steep* I'm not talking your average tilt the wing and turn stuff. I'm talking your getting-thrown-across-the-cockpit-until-your-seatbelt-digs-into-your-gut, worse-than-riding-the-Octopus-at-the-carnival, I-wish-I-hadn't-eaten-all-that-pizza-'cause-it-looks-like-I'm-going-to-be-seeing-it-all-again-real-soon, type of *steep*.

"We're buzzing the landing strip!" the pilot shouted back to me. "We got to scare off all those cows grazing on it!"

"What are cows doing at an airport?" I cried. But as soon as I looked out the window, I realized I'd asked the wrong question. It should have been, "What are we doing landing on a cow pasture?"

Suddenly my life flashed before my eyes. Well, not all of it. That would have been too painful. And the way the plane kept rushing at the ground it looked like I'd be feelin' plenty of pain soon enough. So, instead, I just remembered the part where Dad talked me into all of this . . .

"It'll be great, Son," he had said, slapping his brawny hand on my not-so-brawny back. After I finished coughing to death and checking for broken bones, he continued. "It will show you a whole different part of the world. It'll let you see what other Christians are doing. And most importantly—"

Uh-oh, I thought, *here it comes . . .*

"—it'll teach you to be a real man."

"To be a real man." How many times have I heard that? It seems to be Dad's only concern for my life. Maybe it was because he was All-State something or other in college. Or because I want to be a movie writer when (or if) I ever grow up. Or maybe it's just because I look like Steve Urkel.

In any case, when Dad signed up at church to help build some clinic for a bunch of missionaries in South America, my name mysteriously appeared on the form, too. What a coincidence.

"Cheer up," he said. "It'll be a great week."

Right . . . a whole week of sitting in some hut, slapping flies, and preaching to ignorant savages. I can hardly wait. Don't get me wrong, I'm sure these missionary guys think they've got a life . . .

but seven days without TV, Nintendo, or the mall sounds like seven days of non-stop boredom.

Unfortunately my arguments didn't do much to change Dad's mind. So here I was, up in a little plane diving toward the not-so-little ground. I reached for ol' Betsy, my laptop computer. If we were going down, we'd go down together.

I took one last look out the window. Our little buzz over the pasture did the trick. It scared off the cows. It did a pretty good job of scaring me off, too. But since I didn't have any place to run, I just sat there, strapped into our flying coffin, as we finished circling around for the final approach.

It was late in the day. Below us two or three dozen buildings stood in the low light. Each had brown thatched roofs like something out of Gilligan's Island. Past the buildings was a winding little river, then jungle, more jungle, and . . . you guessed it, even more jungle.

"Keep an eye out for any major holes!" the pilot shouted to Dad, who was sitting beside him in the front seat.

"Got it!" Dad yelled back.

The pilot leveled the plane off, and we started for the pasture.

I guess lots of the natives heard us buzz the field 'cause now they were all running out to watch the show. You can't blame them—they probably enjoy

seeing a good fiery crash as much as civilized
folks. But instead of being naked and carrying
spears, they were all dressed in soccer shorts and
T-shirts. That was good news. It meant they
weren't total savages, which meant, if we survived
the crash, there might be a chance we wouldn't be
eaten.

I stared out the window, watching the field grow
closer and closer, until finally:

*K-RRR-THUMP, BANG, BANG, BUMP, BUMP,
BUMP . . .*

We hit the ground. The pilot fought the steering
wheel for all he was worth.

"DEAD AHEAD!" Dad shouted. "BIG HOLE
DEAD AHEAD!"

The pilot gunned the engine, and we took off a
few feet before coming back down, this time even
harder.

*BUMP, RATTLE-RATTLE, BRUISED GUT,
BRUISED GUT, RATTLE-RATTLE.*

He slammed on the brakes (or whatever pilots
slam on) and we slowed down. It was so bumpy
that we still managed to shake out a few of our
tooth fillings along the way. Finally he turned the
plane around, and we approached the mob of
people racing toward us.

In the lead, riding a motorcycle, was a guy with
a build like Arnold Schwarzenegger. Sitting behind

him was a kid my age—about twelve and pushing thirteen.

"That's Mr. Rodriguez," Dad pointed. "And his son Jamie."

"That's the missionary?" I yelled.

Dad nodded.

"But he's so . . . so . . . "

"*Non*-geeky?" Dad asked.

"Well, yeah . . . "

The pilot shut down the engines, and the people swarmed around the plane as we opened the door. The outside air hit us like a hot, wet blanket.

"It's the humidity." Dad laughed as he saw the expression on my face. He stepped out on the wing and called back, "You'll get used to it."

He climbed down to meet Mr. Rodriguez. The two men threw their arms around each other like they were in a bear hug competition. When they'd finished breaking each other's ribs, Dad turned to make the introductions:

"Paulo, this is my son Wally. Wally, my good friend, Paulo Rodriguez."

We shook hands. I don't want to say that the guy's grip was strong, I just hoped that in a couple of weeks I'd be able to use my fingers again.

Mr. Rodriguez turned to the kid next to him. "And this is my son Jamie."

The kid and I stood for a moment checking each other out. Since Jamie had spent his whole life in the jungle and since I was the more intelligent and civilized of the two, I knew it would be up to me to break the ice. "Me Wally," I said with a big forced grin. "You Jamie."

Jamie threw a concerned look up to his dad. Mr. Rodriguez gave an encouraging smile and nodded.

But it was obvious I wasn't getting through to the poor kid.

I pushed up my glasses and tried again. *"Me Wally,"* I said thumping my chest, *"Wally very happy to meet Jamie."*

The boy scrunched up his face in confusion and then shrugged. Finally he motioned to ol' Betsy, which was slung over my shoulder. "Is that a 486?" he asked, "Do you have a CD-ROM? How many K's in your hard drive?"

*   *   *   *   *

The walk down the dirt road to Jamie's house was like a giant parade—with us as the main attraction. But instead of fancy horses and marching bands, we had squealing pigs and clucking chickens.

Everybody clamored around us. Little kids fought to carry our baggage, and older ones checked out my clothes to see what was in fashion. (I didn't have the heart to tell them that I was a Dork-oid, which meant I was at least two years out of style in everything, including life. But I wasn't worried. I figured they'd find out soon enough.)

I was right. It had taken Jamie only 7.8 seconds to realize he was cooler than me. No biggie for him. But it was for me. It meant I was not only the North American Champion in Dorkiness, but I was probably the South American Champion as well. How exciting! How thrilling! (How embarrassing.)

I also learned that Mr. Rodriguez was a Bible teacher and his wife was a doctor. They'd moved here from Los Angeles about eight years ago and had been working and living with these native types ever since. Now they were building a medical clinic, and Dad and a bunch of other guys from different churches were flying down to help them build it.

"What about you?" Jamie asked. "Are you handy with tools?"

"Me?" I kind of croaked. (Obviously he wasn't as smart as I thought.) I tried to explain. "My older brothers Burt and Brock always pay me to help when they build stuff."

"You're that good?"

"Not exactly—they pay me to stay away."

Jamie laughed. "You sound about as coordinated as me. Instead of helping with the clinic, maybe my dad will let us go upriver and talk to some of the village kids."

"Cool," I said. "What would we talk about?"

"You know—God and stuff."

I felt a cold knot form in my stomach. *Me? Talk about God? To total strangers?*

Before I could point out that I wasn't exactly the next Billy Graham, we turned off the road and into Jamie's front yard.

"WHO GOES THERE, WHO GOES THERE?"

A giant red and yellow parrot raced toward me, flapping his wings and squawking, *"WHO GOES THERE, WHO GOES THERE!"*

"Chill, Millie," Jamie scolded. He turned to me with a shrug. "You'll have to excuse Millie, she's our watch parrot."

"Watch parrot?" I asked.

"Yeah, instead of watch dogs, people down here have watch parrots," he explained. "Sometimes, though, she gets a little neurotic."

"CRAAAWWWK . . . BUT I'M CUTE, BUT I'M CUTE!"

We headed down the walk, stepping over more chickens and pigs, until we finally ducked into the house. The rest of the crowd waved and continued on to their own homes.

Mrs. Rodriguez was as cool as her husband. After going through the usual "How was your trip . . .Would you like something to eat . . . How about something to drink?" routine, Jamie and I were finally able to slip off to his room.

"Wow!" I said as I walked in. "Is this cool or what?" It was like Hollywood meets Disneyland's Jungle Cruise. On the walls were all sorts of movie posters and pictures. Lots of them were autographed by big stars.

"Friends of my folks," Jamie shrugged.

And surrounding the pictures were all sorts of jungle things . . . giant feathers, bracelets of animals' teeth, spears, blowguns, shields made of animal skin.

"Are these all real?" I asked as I dropped my bags and crossed the room toward a nearby spear for a better look.

"Sure," he shrugged again. "Uh, Wally, I wouldn't leave your bags on the floor."

"Why not?"

He pointed to the wooden rafters above us. "Spiders."

I looked up and gasped. There were a couple of critters up on the ceiling. I don't want to say they were big, but I thought I recognized one from an old Japanese science-fiction film.

"Don't worry," Jamie chuckled. "They're not poisonous, but it can be a little surprising when you slip on your pants in the morning and feel them crawling around inside."

"Yeah, right." I smirked, figuring he was joking. The look on his face said he wasn't.

I quickly went back to my bags and tossed them on the bed—all the time keeping a careful eye on the ceiling. It was then I noticed a big white net hanging over my bed. "Hey, what's this thing?" I asked.

"Mosquito netting. It keeps the mosquitoes out . . . and most of the snakes."

"Snakes?" I threw him another terrified look.

He grinned. This time he *was* joking.

"So, uh," I nervously glanced around for any more wildlife as I unzipped my suitcase and started to unpack. "What do you do for fun around here?"

"Oh, the usual . . . swing on vines, outrun cannibals, find ancient treasures in hidden caves."

"No kidding?" I asked excitedly.

"Yes, kidding," he chuckled. (The guy got me again—why didn't somebody tell me I was rooming with a comedian?) "Well, except the part about the hidden caves," he said. "That part's true."

"Really?"

"There's all sorts of legends about hidden gold and jewels and stuff—and spirits that are supposed to guard them."

"Cool. You think we could, like, go explore them or something?"

"Sure," he said, plopping down on the other bed, "but you're only here for a week. I thought you might want to go upriver and minister to some of the local tribes. You know, tell them about—"

Before he went any further, I cut him off. "Listen, uh, Jamie . . . about this ministering stuff . . ." I cleared my throat, feeling a little embarrassed. "I don't think I'm like, you know, cut out to preach at them or any—"

Jamie gave an easy laugh. "Relax, they've already heard about God—lots of 'em are already Christian. They just like to hear about what God's done in your life, that's all."

"I don't know . . ." I hesitated.

"Jamie . . . Wally?" It was Mrs. Rodriguez. "Get washed for supper."

"Okay," Jamie called as he hopped off the bed. Then, turning back to me, he continued. "Look, I don't want to push you into anything. We don't have to go upriver. If you just want to chill a few days, that's cool. Maybe we can go check out those caves, instead."

"Yeah," I agreed. "Buried treasure, that's more my style."

He gave a nod and started toward the door. I followed.

"Uh, Wally, you might want to close up your bags."

"The spiders?" I asked, throwing a nervous look up to the rafters.

"No, the cockroaches."

Chapter 2

Techno Boy to the Rescue

Sitting around eating supper wasn't bad. Well, except the eating part. I kinda like to know what I'm putting into my mouth . . . and mangoes, manioc, yucca, and paca are not the stuff you normally pig out on at the local Golden Arches. I mean, if I could barely say their names, how could I be expected to eat them?

Jamie's sense of humor wasn't much help. Telling me they were monkey brains, pigs' feet, and ant eggs didn't exactly increase my appetite.

Dad and Mr. Rodriguez were a little disappointed that we didn't want to talk to the village kids upriver. They tried to cover it up, but you could tell. It wasn't that I didn't love God and all that, but talking to total strangers about Him, well, it just wasn't my style.

When Jamie brought up the caves, his dad hesitated a moment, but finally gave his permission.

"Just go to the safe ones," he stressed. "Stay away from the ceremonial ones."

"Sure," Jamie agreed. "No sweat."

"Ceremonial ones?" I asked as we headed back to our room to get ready for bed.

"Yeah, weird stuff happens around them. It's best foreigners stay away."

"What do you mean, 'weird'?"

"You know . . ." he hopped into his bed and began pulling the mosquito netting down around him. "Demons, spirits—that kinda stuff. They're everywhere. Well, good night, Wally. Sweet dreams."

SWEET DREAMS!? Fat chance!

In order to dream you have to sleep. And, at the moment, sleep was not at the top of my list. Other than the spiders, snakes, and cockroaches, I now had to worry about "spirits"! No way was I going to sleep. At least not right away. I planned to put it off for a little while . . . like maybe for the rest of my trip!

After a few minutes, they shut down the generator outside, and all the lights in the village went out. I mean *all*. It got dark . . . real dark.

I reached over and pulled ol' Betsy in closer. (Hey! Some kids have teddy bears, I have my laptop.) I opened the lid, turned on a switch, and waited for the screen to light up. Ah, there it was, that wonderful, comforting, blue-green glow.

Maybe a little superhero story would help me relax. Let's see . . .

"RING-RING, RING-RING!"
Techno Boy hops out of his luxurious bath of 30-weight motor oil, rolls on his tank-tread feet across the white carpet (sorry about the stains, Mom) and plugs his finger into the nearest telephone outlet.
"Hello?" he answers.
"Knock, knock," a voice shouts.
"What?"
"Knock, knock," the voice repeats.
"Who's there?" our hero asks puzzled.
"Idaho."
"Idaho who?"
"Idahon't want to tell you this, but we're in a heap of trouble!" Suddenly the voice on the other end breaks into uncontrollable laughter.
"Mr. Mayor?" Techno Boy cries, "Mr. Mayor, is that you?!"
"Ho-ho . . . Ha-ha . . . hee-hee . . ."
"Mr. Mayor, get a grip on yourself!"
"I'm sorry, Techno Boy, it's just that, ho-ho-ha-ha-ha, we've been invaded

by creatures from outer space. They're zapping our entire planet with a Comedy Beam!"

"A Comedy Beam?" Techno Boy cries. "You're joking!"

"Of course," the Mayor laughs. "Everybody's joking! That's the problem. We can't help ourselves. Hee-hee-hee. Say, did you hear about the woman who swallowed a roll of film just to see what would develop? Haa-haa-haa-ho-ho."

"Mr. Mayor! Mr. Mayor!!"

"I'm sorry, Techno Boy, hee-hee-ho-ho, there's nothing we can do. But the beam only affects human minds, not printed circuits. And since you're half computer, you are the only one who can save the day. Say, what's black and white and red all over?"

"What's that, Sir?"

"A blushing penguin! Ho-ho-ho-ho. Hurry, Techno Boy, it's getting worse! By the way, did you know that last night I dreamed I shot an elephant in my pajamas?"

"I'm hanging up now, Sir."

"How he got in my pajamas, I'll never know! Har-har-har . . ."

"Good-bye, Sir." Techno Boy unplugs his finger from the outlet.

Ever since that fiery rocket crash when the government rebuilt his body using rubber bands, paper clips, and any top-secret computer equipment lying around (plus spare parts from some General's 1974 Buick), Techno Boy had dedicated his superpowers to Truth and Justice.

But this . . . How can Techno Boy possibly fight space creatures with comedy beams and—

"Greetings, Earthling."

His ultra-sonic ears pick up a radio transmission tuned to his exact frequency.

"Resistance is futile," the voice says. "Turn yourself over to us, and we will put you to good use—perhaps as a coffee pot or microwave oven."

Quicker than you can say, "This is definitely one of Wally's weirdest stories," Techno Boy drops into first gear, lays a patch of rubber on Mom's carpet, and roars out the door.

Outside, it's worse than he feared. The entire planet is bathed in a light

greener than the mold on your sandwich
after leaving it in your locker over
spring break. Everyone's out in the
street wearing lamp shades, sticking
pencils up their noses, and telling
"knock, knock" jokes.

Above them hovers the menacing spaceship shooting out its dastardly beam.

"Hey, Techno Boy, why do elephants
paint their toenails red?"

Our hero swivels around on his ball-
bearing hips to see Linda Lottahype, TV
reporter for KRUD-TV (and part-time en-
cyclopedia salesperson). Techno Boy is
surprised to notice that this older
woman of great seriousness (and several
layers of makeup) is wearing a party hat
and blowing a noisemaker.

"Ms. Lottahype!" Techno cries. "Not
you, too?"

"We're all under their power." She
giggles. "But you didn't answer my question. Why do elephants paint their toenails red?"

"I don't know." Our hero sighs as he
ducks the noisemaker she keeps blowing
into his face. "Why do elephants paint
their toenails red?"

"To hide in cherry trees! Ha-ha-ha!"

"No offense, Ms. Lottahype, but that's the dumbest joke I've ever —"

"Hey," she interrupts, "have you ever seen an elephant in a cherry tree?"

"Well, no, but —"

"Then, painting their toenails works!"

The poor lady is about to split a gut. She doubles over in laughter, barely able to breathe.

"Ms. Lottahype, Ms. Lottahype, are you okay?"

"Techno Boy, you've gotta help us," she gasps, "you've gotta —"

Suddenly they are interrupted by a loud buzzing. But this is no party noisemaker. This is a giant tractor beam pulling them off the ground and toward the spacecraft. And not just them. Every citizen in the town is being lifted into the air and sucked toward the giant spaceship.

Quickly Techno Boy flips through the channels in his channel-selector brain. At one time he could only pick up stations as far as Toledo, but now that he has installed cable, he can pick up anything, anywhere (well, except for

MTV—after all, he does have some taste).

It's just as he suspected. It's happening everywhere. Every town has a
spaceship above it. Every citizen of
every city is being taken prisoner.
They're all floating hundreds of feet in
the air and being drawn closer and closer
into the ships' monstrous bellies.

What will our microchip marvel do? How
will he defeat this formidable foe? How
can he make the world a safer, saner
(but probably not as funny) place to
live?

Stay tuned, dear reader. As soon as I
get that figured out, I'll be getting
back to you.

*   *   *   *   *

"You didn't tell me it was going to rain!" I
shouted as the water pounded upon my head and
shoulders.

"Why do you think they call it a rain forest?"
Jamie shouted back.

"They should call it a waterfall forest! This is
crazy!"

The rain poured so hard and thick it was almost
impossible to breathe. It was like standing in my

bathroom shower and looking straight up into the nozzle (without, of course, the usual pounding on the door by my sister to hurry . . . or Burt and Brock flushing the toilet to cut back on the cold water pressure so I'd fry).

We'd been walking (or sloshing) about two hours. And the jungle was just as incredible now as when we started. . . .

First, there were the smells. One minute, it was sweeter than when Dad overuses the air freshener in the bathroom—the next, more rotten than my gym socks after five days of non-stop action.

Then, there were the sounds. When it wasn't raining (all twenty seconds' worth), we could hear amazing bird calls and the screaming of monkeys high in the treetops. We could only hear them; we could never see them.

And, speaking of seeing . . . the trees towered hundreds of feet over our heads. Long vines hung from the branches and huge ferns grew from the ground. There were lots of weird-looking berries and flowers. And, at one place on the path, we stopped to watch a thousand yellow and green butterflies fluttering their wings like a giant, living carpet.

But that was only the beginning. . . .

"Wally, hold up a minute!"

I looked down. A snake no bigger than a giant worm wiggled across the path in front of me.

"No biggie," I said, kneeling down for a closer look. After a couple of hours in the forest I figured I was like an expert. Besides, it was so small. What could it possibly do to me?

"What's it called?" I asked.

"A 'Ten Stepper.'"

"Oh, really?" I said, leaning in for a closer look. "Why's that?"

"'Cause after it bites you, you can only run ten steps before dying."

"Augh!" I jumped back and grabbed a nearby vine to keep my balance. At least, I thought it was a vine. But vines aren't supposed to squirm and wiggle.

"Uh, Wally . . . that's a baby boa you're hanging on to."

"AUGH!" I screamed again, letting go of the snake and stumbling backward into a thicket of ferns.

"Wally, I wouldn't go in there if I were—"

But he was too late. My famous McDoogle grace had already kicked into gear. I had fallen and was now lying spread eagle on my back staring straight up into . . .

"A Martian!" I screamed. "It's a Martian!"

The outer-space alien rose to his feet and brandished his deadly claws. His mutant ears stuck straight out, and his long black mouth opened and closed in eager anticipation. I was petrified . . . and a little put out with God. I mean, if I were going to be kidnaped by space creatures, why couldn't it be at home where I could at least get it on video tape and maybe grab a snack for the road?

The monster lunged toward me.

Suddenly Jamie appeared. He hit the alien hard with a rotten log. The creature went flying. Before he had a chance to get back to his feet and draw his ray gun, Jamie hit him again, then again.

"Get outta here! Shoo! Go home! Go home!"

The alien finally turned and lumbered off—no doubt to get reinforcements back at his spaceship.

"You okay?" Jamie asked as he helped me to my feet.

"Wow!" I gasped.

"Stupid anteaters."

"Anteater?" I asked.

"Yeah, they're all over the place."

"Anteaters?"

Again Jamie nodded.

I breathed a sigh of relief and realized I better cut back on writing my little fantasies—they were definitely having an effect on me.

"Hey, check it out," Jamie said. "Look at all the bat droppings on the ground."

"Bat droppings?" I repeated.

Yeah, that means there's a major cave right around here."

"What do caves have to do with bats?"

"That's where bats live."

"Bats live where we're going?" I asked.

"Sure, thousands of 'em—come on."

I threw a longing look back to where the ant-eater had run off. Maybe being abducted by an alien space creature wasn't such a bad deal after all.

Chapter 3

Hello in There . . .

Suddenly the entrance to the cave appeared. With all the ferns and trees and vines, you wouldn't even have seen it . . . except for the bat droppings all around—and the trampled mud.

"Looks like shoe prints," Jamie said as he stooped down to examine the soggy dirt. "Lots of 'em."

"Human?" I asked nervously. Somehow I figured bats didn't wear Reeboks, but I wasn't so sure about those spirit things.

"Of course, 'human,'" Jamie said. "C'mon." He pulled a flashlight out of his backback and started toward the cave.

I wanted to follow, but my legs weren't exactly in the mood. It probably had something to do with the way my knees were knocking. "Uh . . . Jamie? . . ."

He turned back to me.

"About those bats . . . uh, they don't, like, hurt people, do they?"

"Not unless they're vampires."

I broke into a grin. "Yeah, right . . ."

He wasn't grinning back.

"Come on," I laughed, "there's no such thing as vampires."

Still no grin.

"Are there?"

Jamie shrugged. "Not like in the movies, but there are some small bats that bite animals and suck their blood."

I swallowed hard and peered into the cave. "You think there are any in there?"

"Nah," he said, turning and entering.

I sighed in relief.

"The evil spirits scare 'em away."

"Now cut that out!" I cried as he broke out laughing.

"Sorry," he said.

The first thing I noticed when we were inside was the smell. It reminded me of something that had died . . . in an outhouse . . . smothered in rotten eggs . . . and covered with a generous layer of limburger cheese. (Either that or my little sister's cooking. It was hard to tell the difference.)

In any case, it was so strong that it overloaded my nose and made me start to sneeze. "*Ah . . . Ahh*

. . . AHH-CHOO!" Then again, *"Ah . . . Ahh . . . AHH-CHOO."* And again, *"AH-CHOO!"*

Between sneezes, I noticed a few things. Like how cold the cave was. It was a good ten to twenty degrees cooler inside than out.

I also noticed the rain . . . or lack of it. Everything was very, very quiet. Well, except for the occasional *AH-CHOOs!*

Finally, I noticed the floor of the cave. It was moving. Strange. There was no stream. No wind blowing sand around. So why was the floor movi—

"Insects," Jamie answered, reading my mind as he flashed the light down to them. "Mostly insects and grubs . . . though it looks like there are a few rats around, too."

"Okay," I said turning back to the entrance, "that wraps up my cave exploring. *AH-CHOO!*"

"Wait a minute," he said, grabbing my arm. "Look at that!"

"Jamie, listen, I, uh . . . I think I can catch most of this kind of stuff back home on the TV Discovery Channel, so if you don't mind—"

"Over there," Jamie said, shining his light beam through the darkness.

Common sense told me to keep going. To run out of there and catch the next bus home . . .

Home: where the only bats you see belong to baseball teams.

Home: where you can always find a nice, dry,
       AH-CHOO! Kleenex.
Home: where the only time the floor moves is
       when you have a good, old-fashioned,
       dependable earthquake.

That's what common sense said. So, of course I
ignored it and turned to see what Jamie was pointing to. At first I saw nothing. Then I noticed it. A
tiny reflection at the far end of the cave.

"C'mon," Jamie whispered.

"What about the bugs?"

"Just slide your feet—most of 'em will get out of
your way."

"*Most* of 'em?" I asked. "What about *the rest* of
them?"

But he'd already started off.

"Jamie! Jamie, wait for—*AH-CHOO!*" I managed to grab his sleeve and began scooting my feet
behind him. Already I could hear some crunches
and squishes, but I had no desire to look down and
see exactly what was crunching and squishing.
Somehow I already knew there were going to be
lots of little bug families heartbroken that Daddy
bug wouldn't be making it home that night.

As my eyes got adjusted to the dark, I could see
large stone pillars rising from the floor. "Stalag-
mites," Mr. Reptenson, my science teacher, called
them. That meant that above them there would be

. . . I looked up. Yup, there they were—long, pointed, "stalactites." Only, like the floor, these little icicles of rock were moving.

"Uh, Jamie . . ."

"It's just the bats," he interrupted. "They sleep during the day. Don't worry, you're perfectly safe."

Sure. What did I have to worry about? Living floors, living ceilings, not-so-living spirits, mysterious glowing objects in pitch black caves. Sounded perfectly safe to me.

We were closer to the reflection now. Much closer.

"It's a sheet of plastic," Jamie half whispered. "But what's a sheet of plastic doing—"

"*STRAW-EEEK!!*

I leaped out of my skin and onto Jamie's back.

"*STRAW-EEEK!! STRAWK-EEEK!!*

"It's a Guacharo," Jamie said, trying to pry me loose. "Wally, will you get off? Wally. WALLY!" But it did no good. I stuck to him tighter than month-old chewing gum under a desk. "It's just an oil bird, Wally. Will you please get off? We frightened him a little, that's all."

"*We* frightened *him?*" I cried. "What does he think he did to us?"

"Wally . . . please . . ."

I finally climbed back down to the ground.

We arrived at the plastic, and Jamie carefully pulled it aside. "Look at that!"

I leaned forward. *"AH-CHOO!"* It was a pile of something, but I couldn't make it out. "What is it?"

He bent down for a closer look. "Skins . . ."

"I'm sorry, what?"

"Poachers."

"Mind if we talk English?"

"These are jaguar skins. Somebody's hiding them here."

"Why?"

"It's illegal to hunt animals. It's like a national law."

I started to understand. "So somebody's, somebody's *AHH-CHOO!* . . ."

Jamie finished my thought. "Some poachers are killing jaguars for their skins and storing them in here."

"You mean this is like a bad guy's hideout?" I asked.

"I'm afraid so."

"Great," I muttered, "just great." I was about to ask Jamie if this was a typical day in his life or if he was just showing me a good time, when suddenly we heard:

"WHO'S THERE?"

Jamie quickly snapped off his light as another beam glanced off the wall beside us.

"Get down," Jamie whispered.

We ducked as the light swept above us, barely missing our heads.

"I SAID, WHO'S THERE?" the gruff voice demanded.

"Over here!" Jamie whispered to me as he pointed to a nearby stalagmite. It was big enough for us to hide behind. We quietly moved to it and just in time.

The voice and light started to approach. "If there's somebody in here, ya better come out!"

Then there was another voice: "What's the problem, Hector?"

And a third: "Somebody gonna give me a hand with this animal?"

Great, I thought, *just what we need, a bad guy convention.*

The footsteps came closer . . . so did the light. The beam swept all around, barely missing us, as we scrunched closer to the cold stone.

"Just stay still," Jamie whispered.

"I wasn't planning on doing aerobics," I mumbled.

The second voice entered the cave and turned on his flashlight. "I don't see nothin'," he said as he shot his beam all around the floor and back wall.

"I thought for sure I heard somethin'," the first voice insisted. He came a couple of steps closer, still searching.

We gradually edged around the stone just to make sure he couldn't see us. Everything was fine ... well, except for my nose. It had started to tickle again. I took a quick gasp. Jamie spun around and glared at me. I tried to hold it back. My eyes started to water. My lip started to tremble. But there was no stopping it. Another sneeze was on its way.

"*Ahhh ...*"

"Somebody give me a hand with this animal," the third voice demanded from outside the cave. "It's heavy!"

"*AHHH ...*" I could tell it was going to be a good one. "Grab your nose!" Jamie whispered.

I grabbed my nose. I figured I'd probably blow my brains through my ears when I sneezed, but no biggie. We were goners, anyway. Then suddenly, the urge passed, just like that. I couldn't believe it. Grabbing my nose had actually stopped the sneeze!

"Come on!" the third voice repeated. "Now!"

"All right, all right ..." the other two voices complained, "we're coming, we're coming." They shuffled away from us and toward the opening.

Jamie and I exchanged grins. Sweet victory. I let go of my nose.

"*AHHHH-CHOOOOOOO!*"

It was the biggest sneeze in the history of the world.

Suddenly both flashlights spun around and landed squarely on us.

"THERE THEY ARE!"

"RUN!" Jamie cried as he leaped to his feet.

He didn't have to worry. I was right behind him.

The first man moved to block our path, but the cave floor was so slick that he immediately went crashing to the ground.

"My leg!" he screamed. "My leg!"

The second guy was not nearly as clumsy, but he was a whole lot uglier. He had a jagged scar from the side of his ear all the way down to his mouth. In a flash he reached out and grabbed Jamie.

"LET ME GO!" Jamie shouted. "LET ME GO!"

I raced at ol' Scar Face with everything I had. Which, if you're the world's greatest wimp, really isn't that much. But as the guy tried to snatch me with his free hand, he let go of Jamie just enough so the kid could tromp down on his foot with all his might!

"YEOW!" the man cried. He grabbed his foot. "OH, MY!" he screamed, hopping up and down. "WHAT A RATHER UNPLEASANT EXPERI-ENCE THIS HAS BECOME!" (Actually, that's not really what he said, but since I'm a Christian, I probably shouldn't use his real words.)

"STOP THEM!" the first man cried, as he scrambled to his feet, took a couple of hops, then slipped and fell again. "STOP THEM!"

We raced out of the cave and into the daylight. Two down, one to go. Unfortunately the "one" was the size of a small house. In his arms was a dead leopard, which he quickly dropped so he could lunge at us.

Jamie faked to the left and spun to the right like an NFL pro. I, on the other hand, used all of my great athletic skill and coordination to run smack dab into the big man's arms.

"GOTCHA!" he cried.

"LET GO OF ME!" I cried. "LET GO OF ME!"

But it did no good. He just hung on tighter. "So you thought you'd steal our skins, did you?"

And then it happened—another sneeze started.

"Ahh . . ."

I looked up to him. He glared down at me with a hatred that said we'd probably never become best buddies.

"AHH . . ."

Now, normally, I know it's polite to cover your mouth when you sneeze. But since, at the moment, both of my arms were kinda pinned to my side, there wasn't much I could do.

"AHHHH-CHOOOO!!" I let go with the second biggest sneeze in recorded history (the biggest was back on page 32) . . . directly into the burly man's face.

"AAAWWCK . . ." the big guy cried as he dropped me to wipe off his face.

That's all it took. With a polite "Excuse me" (Mom always taught me to be polite), I raced after Jamie for all I was worth!

"STOP THEM! GET THOSE TWO *'BLANKETY-BLANK'* BRATS!"

Neither Jamie nor I thought now was a good time to stop and tell them that there were children present and they should clean up their language. Especially since all three were considering even worse sins . . . like murder!

So we just kept running—ferns and vines flying in our faces. There were no paths where we were going. Come to think of it, *where were we going?*

I don't suppose it mattered where we headed 'cause with every step Broken Leg, Scar Face, and Big Guy were gaining on us.

Then I saw it. Up ahead, through the bushes . . . the river.

Great, that meant Jamie knew a shortcut. He must be heading toward a bridge where we can cross the river and—

Suddenly Jamie dropped out of sight. What on earth? When I finally saw the reason, it was too late. I also dropped.

"AUGHHHHHHHHHHHHHHHHhhhhhh . . . !"

KER-SPLASH!

So much for shortcuts and bridges.

Chapter 4

A Little River Cruise

I don't know how long I was under water, but I guess it wasn't long enough. 'Cause when I came back up, coughing and choking, the three men were standing high above us on the bank shouting and cursing. They were not wild about our unexpected visit and even less thrilled about our hasty exit. But it was the fact that we had seen their faces and could identify them that really ruined their day.

"YOU COME BACK HERE!" they screamed. "COME BACK HERE! WE CAN WORK THINGS OUT!"

Neither Jamie nor I thought we should take them up on the invitation. If they really wanted to talk, they could just jump in and join us for a swim. But for some reason they didn't. Instead, they just walked along the bank shouting their lungs out as the current carried us downstream.

"I hope you can swim!" Jamie yelled over his shoulder to me.

"No need," I called back. "My feet can touch the bottom."

"Uh, I wouldn't do that, Wally."

"Why not?

"Stingrays—they sleep on the bottom. They're not real keen about getting stepped on."

I pulled up my feet. "Is that why those guys didn't jump in after us?"

"Nah," Jamie said. "They're just afraid of the piranha."

"Piranha? What's that?" Somehow I already suspected the worse.

"Man-eating fish."

"*MAN-EATING FISH!?*"

"Yeah, but usually they just attack smaller animals."

"*USUALLY??*"

"It's the crocodiles we gotta watch out for."

"*CROCODILES!?*" I was beginning to sound like an echo.

"I'd keep my eyes open for them, if I were you."

By now the current was moving so fast the guys on the bank couldn't keep up. They did, however, manage to squeeze in a few last-minute threats, and plenty of cursing, before they turned and raced back into the jungle.

"That was a lot of fun," I scorned, as I rolled onto my back to float and rest a minute. I wasn't the world's greatest swimmer, but as long as I could float I did pretty good. "What's next? Wrestling with gorillas? Outrunning lions?"

"Don't be silly," Jamie said, "they don't have gorillas or lions in South America."

If that was supposed to be comforting it didn't help.

We floated along for several minutes. The water wasn't chilly. It was more like bath water. Actually, because of all the mud and stuff in it, it was more like soup. Heavy, brown, bean-with-bacon-soup . . . with us as the bacon.

I was about to ask Jamie how much farther, when he pointed toward the shore. "Hey, check it out," he said.

The high bank had dropped down to a little beach. A long, brown log rested on it. It was half in the water and half out. Without a word he started swimming toward it.

I followed. But as the water grew more shallow, I grew more nervous. The last thing I wanted to do was wake one of those stingray guys from their afternoon nap. (If they're anything like Dad, they'd definitely wake up on the cranky side.)

"Don't worry," Jamie said, once again reading my mind. He rose to his feet. The water was about waist deep now. "Just shuffle your feet and splash around. They'll hear you and take off."

I got to my feet and did just that. Actually, a lot of 'just that'—a *whole* lot.

"What are you doing?" Jamie laughed.

"I want them to think we're a herd of elephants dropping by," I said as I kept splashing and kicking.

"Elephants are in Africa and Asia."

"All right, hippopotamuses."

"Guess again."

"Okay, okay, then a whole clan of polar bears that have come down from Alaska on their spring break so they can go back home and impress everyone with their cool tans."

Jamie chuckled as we finally arrived at the log. But it wasn't a log.

"It's a canoe," I cried.

"Yeah, a dugout," Jamie answered as he looked inside. "The Indians burn and dig out the middle of these long logs to make them into dugouts."

"No kidding."

"Yeah, only this doesn't belong to any Indian."

"How can you tell?"

"Check out the duffel bag—and the radio." He pointed to a nylon gym bag and walkie-talkie at the far end of the boat. "And look at these shoeprints along the beach. They're exactly the same as in front of the cave."

"You mean this belongs to those poacher guys?" I asked.

"I'd bet my life on it."

I wished he hadn't worded it that way. "Uh, listen, Jamie," I said, glancing around nervously. "This has been a lot of fun and everything, but shouldn't we, like, be getting back?"

"My thoughts exactly."

"Good." I started to slosh up onto the shore.

He grabbed my arm, "But I wouldn't go that way."

"Why not?"

"Those guys know the village is upriver. They know we'd have to cross past them to get back."

I stopped. "You mean, they'll be waiting for us?"

"Poaching's a serious crime," he said. "I'm sure they'll do anything they can to stop us from telling the authorities."

"Anything?"

Jamie nodded.

I swallowed hard. By anything I knew he wasn't talking about just any ol' anything. He was talking the *big* anything. The anything where you don't exactly make it home in time for dinner—or for the rest of your life.

"Can't we just keep going downriver till we get to civilization?" I asked.

Jamie shook his head. "There's nothing for miles. And what tribes there are . . . well, they

prefer to be left alone. They get kinda unpredictable toward outsiders."

I swallowed again. *Unpredictable* sounded like
a polite word for *un*friendly . . . which sounded to
me like another opportunity to become *un*alive.

"So," Jamie sighed. "We can't go downriver, and
we can't go upriver . . . at least by foot." He glanced
back to the dugout. I could see the idea forming.

"Oh, no," I protested, "No way are we stealing
their canoe!"

"Wally—"

"If we steal their canoe," I argued, "they'll be
twice as mad."

"So what are they going to do, kill us twice as
many times?" he asked. "Don't you see, if we take
their dugout, we can paddle upstream. We can
stay in the middle of the river so they won't be able
to get us."

"They can swim," I argued.

"And we can paddle," he said as he started to
climb in. "Come on."

"Jamie . . ."

"Come on."

I threw a look back into the jungle. I wasn't crazy
about ripping off their canoe, but I was even less
crazy about them ripping off my life. "All right," I
said, climbing out of the water and into the dugout,
"but if we die, you're going to live to regret it."

As I stepped into the dugout, it tipped violently to the left. "WHOA!" I shouted, trying to keep my balance. But it was too late, I went flying into the water with a loud:

KER-SPLASH!

When I came up Jamie was laughing. "These things are kinda tricky," he explained. "You've got to be careful where you put your weight."

I stood up and tried again. Carefully I stepped inside the narrow little boat. It still tipped, but Jamie was inside leaning the other way to keep it steady.

"It's probably best if you just sit down in the middle," he explained. He pulled out a long pole lying inside the dugout. "I'll do the pushing."

I watched as he carefully dug the stick into the riverbed and pushed us off—all the time, straddling the dugout with a foot on each edge, keeping perfect balance.

"Where are the paddles?" I asked.

"You're looking at it," he said referring to his stick. "They use these poles to push them wherever they're going." He stuck the pole into the bottom of the river and pushed again . . . then again. Soon we were in the center of the river. I was kind of jealous to see how effortlessly Jamie kept his balance, while at the same time easily pushing us up the river.

"Where'd you learn that?" I asked.

"Kids out here can steer a dugout before they can run." Jamie grinned. "You guys have your bicycles and skateboards, we have our dugouts." Suddenly Jamie's grin disappeared.

"What's wrong?" I asked following his gaze. Then I saw them. Three men in a dugout coming toward us, fast. But they weren't just any three men. They were our three men!

"I thought *this* was their dugout!" I cried.

"It is!" Jamie yelled as he quickly spun us around and started down the river. "Looks like they had two!"

"Where are we going?" I shouted. "You're not taking us *downriver*!"

"I'm open to suggestions!" he yelled as he kept pushing and we began picking up speed.

I glanced over my shoulder. They were gaining on us. "But downriver," I said turning back to him, "you said there were unfriendly Indians downriver."

"I didn't say unfriendly," Jamie kept pushing with his pole as the current swept us faster and faster. "I said 'unpredictable!' People haven't spent much time with them—we don't know what they're like."

By now we'd made it into the swiftest part of the river. We began moving faster than Jamie could push. Now all he could do was steer. It was about that time I noticed a faint roar. But I didn't have time to pay attention. I was too busy looking over my shoulder and praying.

"With any luck," Jamie shouted, "those guys will chicken out and stop following us."

"Because of the Indians?" I asked.

"Well, partly, yeah."

I hated to ask, but I knew I had to. "What's the other reason?" I guess he didn't hear me. He was concentrating pretty hard on steering us toward the bank. Also, the roar was getting louder. I tried again. "Why would they chicken out, Jamie? JAMIE?"

"Because of the water—!"

I couldn't hear the last word. The roar was much louder, now. "What?" I shouted. "Because of the what?"

"Because of the waterfall!"

"What waterfall?"

He pointed ahead. "That one!"

I craned my neck. There was no waterfall. There were a few rocks here and there. Granted, they looked kind of dangerous as we zipped past them, but I saw no waterfall.

I threw a questioning look to Jamie, then back to the river. Up ahead there were only rocks, river, sky and . . . Wait a minute. There wasn't supposed to be sky there. There was supposed to be river

there. What happened to our river? Suddenly it
dawned on me Jamie might have a point.

"JAMIE!" I shouted, "GET US OUT OF HERE!"

"I'M TRYING!" Jamie yelled as he kept pushing
with his pole, struggling to guide us toward the
bank. The roar was deafening now. I could see
mist rising from the edge of the river just a dozen
yards ahead of us.

I stuck my hand into the water and started pad-
dling. "WHAT CAN I DO?" I cried, "WHAT CAN I
DO?"

"PRAYING WOULD BE NICE!"

I threw a look back over my shoulder. The bad
guys were making a beeline to the shore. They
were going to be okay. I looked up ahead. We'd run
out of water. We *weren't* going to be okay. "Dear
God," I quickly mumbled as I took off my glasses
and shoved them into my pants pocket. "I know
you're kinda busy these days with wars and fam-
ines and all, but if it's not too much bother would
You mind, like, saving our liv—"

"HANG ON!" Jamie shouted.

Our dugout shot over the edge. For a moment
we seemed to float in midair, you know, like in
those cartoons. Like just before Wiley Coyote drops
from the Roadrunner's sight and gets smashed to
smithereens.

Smashed to smithereens?!

I prayed harder but was suddenly interrupted when the front of the dugout dipped forward and dropped. There was the river, a zillion miles below. We began a perfect, 100-miles-per-hour nose dive toward it. I wanted to finish my prayer, but something else came to mind. Something like:

"AUGHHHHHHHHHHHHHHHHHHHHHHH HHHHHHHHHHHH!!!!!!!"

As far as screams went, it was pretty good. But it didn't seem to help much. Everything turned to slow motion as we continued to fall and fall and then fall some more. (If I knew it was going to take this much time, I'd have brought ol' Betsy along and finished my story.)

Finally we hit the water and went under. I began tumbling around and around. I opened my eyes. All I saw were bubbles and water as I kept turning over and over. It probably would have been a lot of fun except for the part about breathing . . .

I couldn't.

I had to get some air. I started toward the surface, then remembered one tiny detail—with all the tumbling I didn't know where the surface was.

Things were getting desperate. My lungs were beginning to burn, and I was continuing to tumble. I had to get some air, but I didn't know which direction to go. Still, any direction was better than staying in this perpetual spin cycle.

I began kicking and swimming for all I was worth. My lungs were on fire. I had to find the surface. And then I saw it. A giant boulder. Well, at least that broke up the monotony of water and bubbles. The only problem was the current seemed to be pushing me toward that boulder awfully fast. The only problem was I couldn't seem to find the brakes. The only problem was . . .

KLUNK!

Suddenly there were no problems. Suddenly there was nothing. . . .

Chapter 5

Guess Who's for Dinner?

I thought I was dreaming. Where else but in a dream would you see a two-headed monster staring down at you? The first head looked exactly like it belonged to a normal boy. Well, except for the red goop smeared all over his hair . . . and the black paint around his eyes.

I looked over to the second head. Now it's true, I wasn't wearing my glasses, but even with my foggy vision that second head looked exactly like . . . I blinked . . . exactly like . . . a monkey.

"You okay, Wally?" Now Jamie leaned into my view. He was also looking down at me. Luckily, he only had one head. "Wally, are you all right?"

I tried to nod, but the pain shooting through my skull said that wasn't such a hot idea.

"Just lie quietly," Jamie said. "You got a nasty bump on your noggin."

I blinked again and looked back to the monster's second head (the one that looked like a monkey). Without warning it leaped off the monster's shoulders and began jumping around on the ground.

I screamed.

The monkey screamed.

I screamed louder.

The monkey screamed louder, still.

Figuring he wanted to play hardball, I blasted him with everything I had. (For a nightmare this was getting pretty bizarre . . . and noisy.) My screaming did the trick. The monkey scampered back onto the boy's shoulder where he belonged. Then it dawned on me. This was no nightmare. He wasn't a two-headed monster. He was just your average cannibal type boy with his average cannibal type pet. Immediately, I worried if I was about to become his average cannibal type meal.

"Here," Jamie said, holding the end of a long branch over my mouth. "Open up."

"What is it?" I croaked.

"An Igapa tree—they store rainwater."

I hesitated.

"Come on, it's perfectly safe and you need some liquid."

After my wrestling bout with the waterfall, I figured "liquid" was the last thing I needed, but I obeyed anyway. Keeping one eye on the monkey, who was still pretty sore over losing our shouting match, and the other eye on the new kid, I opened my mouth. The water tasted sweet, and I drank it as fast as I could.

"Easy," Jamie said. "Not so fast—easy, now."

"Where are we?" I asked, coughing and gasping between gulps. "And who is *he?*" I pointed to the boy.

"The best I can figure, we kind of got knocked out in our waterfall tumble. I guess this guy here—I call him George—fished us out."

I quit drinking and reached into my pocket. Luckily my glasses were still in one piece. I slipped them on, and the monkey went even crazier than before. I guess he'd never seen someone with four eyes. George was pretty surprised too, but he wasn't afraid. Instead he leaned right into my face, nose to nose, and checked them out.

Now that my vision was clearer (and he was a lot closer), I could see George was about our age. He had thick, black hair with red paste smeared all over the top. Around his eyes was a painted black mask like a raccoon's. He also had some feathered armbands encircling his upper arms.

Oh, and one other thing . . . He was naked! Totally! Well, except for the little string he wore around his waist. It didn't cover much, but at least it was a start.

The way he held in his stomach and pushed out his chest, I got the feeling that he was trying to impress us with his bravery. And for a kid, I guess he was kind of courageous. I mean, meeting a couple of foreigners like us should spook anybody.

When he finished inspecting my glasses, he rose to his feet, grabbed his nearby bow, and started rattling off a bunch of gibberish.

Jamie listened carefully then translated. "I think George wants us to follow," he said as he helped me to my feet.

"Where?" I asked hesitantly.

"I can't tell for certain. He said something about 'his tribe' and 'eating' and 'us.'"

"JAMIE!"

"No, no, no," Jamie laughed. "Not eating *us*. Having us eat *with* him . . . at his village."

"I hope you told him we have other plans."

"Like what—a burger and a movie?"

"Well, no. Like . . . like . . ."

"Like staying out here tonight and getting eaten by a jaguar . . . or getting more lost . . . or getting caught by those goons upriver? . . ."

"Well, no, but, but . . ."

Jamie waited for some type of argument. Unfortunately, *"No, but, but"* was the best I could come up with.

George gave another grunt, turned, and disappeared into the jungle. Jamie quickly followed.

"Jamie . . ." I called. "Jamie . . ."

But it did no good. In a second he'd also vanished. I stood there all alone. It was starting to rain again. It was also getting dark. And since I figured Jamie and George would be scared to be in the dark, rainy jungle all by themselves, I decided to go and keep them company.

"Jamie . . . wait up!"

Now that I was sure we weren't going to be George's dinner, the walk through the jungle wasn't half bad. I was even getting used to the rain—though I kinda envied George for not having to wear soaked clothes that stuck all over his body.

But that wasn't the only thing I envied. As we kept walking, I began to think how neat it must be to live out here—no hassles, no homework, no cat box to empty . . . just you and nature. Talk about the "good life." True, they may not have cable TV or the latest Nintendo Game Boy, but that's a small price to pay for such a cool way of living.

That got me thinking about Jamie . . . and his family. I mean, how can missionaries go around talking to everyone about God? Oh, sure I know

we should tell natives about Jesus and everything
. . . but aren't these people pretty happy just the
way they are?

Suddenly I noticed Jamie and George had stopped
talking. They had been chattering away like old
friends, but now they were quiet. Very quiet.

"Everything okay?" I asked.

Jamie motioned for me to be still.

"Why?" I asked.

He pointed to George who was now moving very
slowly, trying not to make a sound.

I looked around nervously, expecting some killer
animal to leap out from behind the next tree. But
I didn't see a thing. Nothing. Finally I pulled on
Jamie's sleeve and mouthed the words, "What's
the problem?"

"George heard a noise," Jamie whispered. "He
thinks it's his twin sister."

"So why are we whispering?" I asked.

"Because she's been dead eleven years."

I swallowed hard. I had a sneaking suspicion I
wasn't going to like the rest of this conversation.
"How . . . how'd she die?"

"Her parents killed her."

I was right. Still, I had to know more. "W-w-
why?"

"Because they believe twins are bad luck . . . and
because she was a girl."

"That's awful."

Jamie nodded. "It gets worse. They bury their unwanted babies in the ground and leave them there to die."

I could feel my stomach getting kind of queasy. Oh, sure, there were times I'd like to do away with my own sister—but only for a few minutes. Not forever.

"So why are we whispering?" I repeated.

"His family was supposed to burn her body and drink her ashes so she wouldn't come back to hurt them."

If I thought I was sick before, that last bit of news almost did me in.

Jamie continued. "But they didn't, so now everyone lives in fear of her spirit."

I threw a look over to George. What had once been a brave, fearless, wanna-be warrior, now looked like a frightened little kid, all wide-eyed and petrified. It was kinda sad. Even his monkey buddy looked a little nervous.

I turned back to Jamie. "So every time they hear a strange noise, they think it's a spirit?"

Jamie nodded. "They practice all sorts of weird stuff to keep those spirits away."

I didn't want to know what "weird stuff" he was talking about. I'd heard enough. Maybe life in the jungle wasn't so cool after all. Maybe there were

a few things these people needed straightening out
on. I'm sure his twin sister would have thought so.
And by the fear on George's face, he probably
thought so, too.

A few minutes later we pushed aside the last of
the ferns, and there it was . . . George's village.
Hut, sweet hut.

Actually there were nine huts. Big ones, all in a
circle. A tenth one was in the center.

"That's where the men stay," Jamie said, pointing to the middle one. "The single men stay—"

Suddenly an old man jumped in front of us. He
had a huge wooden disk stuck in his lower lip. It
made him look like he was sucking on a Frisbee.

Being the tremendous man of courage that I am,
I only screamed for half a minute:

AUGHHHHHHHHHHHHHHHHH!

(I could have gone longer but I ran out of air. Of
course, Jamie's punch in the gut didn't help much.)

"Knock it off!" he hissed.

But the damage was done. Who needs an alarm
system when you got Chicken Man McDoogle? My
little vocal exercise managed to warn the entire
village. Soon everyone had raced out to see us. Before I knew it, we were right smack in the middle
of a National Geographic special—complete with

women wearing almost no clothing, and men wearing even less. They all circled around us, pointing and jabbering a mile a minute.

The little kids were the bravest. They came right up to us and poked and laughed and giggled. The grownups' courage soon followed. Now everyone was closing in tighter and tighter.

"How's your prayer life?" Jamie whispered.

"Why?"

"Looks like we might need a little help."

At that exact minute, the crowd parted. An older guy with necklaces and a zillion scars across his body walked toward us.

"Is he the chief?" I whispered.

"Sort of," Jamie answered. "He's called a shaman. He's kinda like a witch doctor."

"Who did that to him—cut him up like that with all those scars?" I asked.

"He did."

"What?"

"They burn themselves—sometimes for decoration, but a lot of times to keep the dead spirits happy."

"Ow," I said, wincing at the thought.

By now the shaman had started talking with George. The old-timer was getting pretty worked up. In fact, the whole tribe was getting a little hot under the collar. (A neat trick since they had no collars . . . or shirts, for that matter!)

"Are they mad at us?" I whispered.

"I'm not sure," Jamie frowned, trying to listen. "They're saying something about George's sister and our coming here, but—"

That was as far as Jamie got. Suddenly a bunch of young guys moved forward. They grabbed each of us by our arms and dragged us toward the hut in the middle of the village.

"What's going on?" I shouted as they pulled Jamie ahead of me.

"I can't tell!" Jamie called back. "Either we're their guests or . . ."

He didn't have to say anything else. I swallowed hard. Suddenly a thought came to mind. "You don't think they'll let us call 911, do you?" I shouted.

But Jamie was gone. He was already inside the hut, and I was about to follow. . . .

Chapter 6

Party On

The first thing I noticed in the hut was the smoke. It was awful—worse than stepping into the teacher's lounge back at my school. Well, maybe not that bad, but close. Don't get me wrong, it was kinda cozy seeing a nice fire in the middle of the men's living area, but they seemed to be missing a couple of things . . . like a fireplace and a chimney! I guess they figured the hole at the top of the roof would do the trick. And it did . . . kind of.

Next I noticed there wasn't much furniture. I didn't expect to see a lot of big screen TVs and dinette sets, but a few sofas, or beds, or even a chair would have been nice. There was nothing. Just lots of cotton hammocks strung every which way between the tall supporting posts.

Jamie was already talking with the shaman and his head guys. I figured he was trying to convince them to hold off eating us till dessert, or maybe even breakfast.

"They're trying to protect us," Jamie said as he finally turned to me to explain.

"Protect us?" I asked.

"Yeah, 'cause we're foreigners, they think George's dead sister is going to hurt us. That's why they dragged us into the hut. They don't want to hurt us; they want to protect us."

I glanced over to George and the men. They tried to look brave, but you could see they were kinda scared. It made me feel good knowing they were willing to risk their lives to protect ours— even if there wasn't anything to protect us from.

Or was there?

"Jamie," I said, kind of confused. "There are no such things as ghosts, right?"

"All I know is that when we die, we either go to heaven or hell. Nobody's spirit hangs around here. But I also know that the Bible talks about demons, too. And all of the tribes are, like, totally afraid of them." Jamie shrugged.

"But they can't hurt *us*, right?" It was sort of a statement and sort of a question.

Jamie nodded. "Since we are Christians we can ask Jesus to protect us, but these guys don't know about Jesus."

"No wonder they're scared," I said.

"More like petrified," Jamie agreed. "They're totally controlled by their fear. It's pretty sad."

Jamie was right. As I looked at the faces of the men, it *was* sad. But it was only the beginning . . .

*   *   *   *   *

A couple of hours later we were in the middle of a big circle enjoying a feast (that is, if you call dried fish on a leaf a "feast"). But it was the best they had, and you could tell they were really proud about giving it to us.

Jamie sat on the ground to my left. For a while George and his monkey sat on the other side. We were becoming pretty good buddies—even his monkey was getting friendly. It was a little weird the first time he hopped over to my shoulder, but it was also pretty cool. I could tell he was still curious about my glasses, so I took them off and let him play with them.

When he finally managed to put them on, the little guy went ballistic. Everyone laughed as he leaped around, chattering and bumping into things. (I guess he wasn't used to my 20–200 vision.)

A few minutes later, the shaman and a couple of the head guys came over and started talking with George. Things got pretty heated pretty quick. Whatever they were saying, it was obvious George didn't much like it. But after a few more sharp words from the shaman, George finally nodded and stood up. He called his pet, handed me my glasses, and left without a word. I wasn't sure what had happened or where he was going, but he definitely wasn't smiling.

We sat around the fire listening to the older guys talk and act out some pretty tall hunting tales. You could tell everything was exaggerated by about a hundred times, but that made it all the more fun.

Meanwhile, Jamie was learning all sorts of things from the shaman—mostly how the tribe was in the middle of a giant epidemic of yellow fever or dysentery or some sort of disease. Whatever it was, it was making a lot of them sick and killing them off left and right. Jamie recognized the symptoms and explained to the shaman that his folk's medical clinic back at the village had a cure for the disease.

"That's great," I said when he stopped to translate for me. "So you're gonna, like, vaccinate them, right?"

Jamie shook his head.

"Why not?"

"He won't let us," Jamie said motioning toward the shaman.

"You're kidding!"

Jamie sighed. "He thinks it's the spirits that are killing them, not the disease."

I couldn't believe my ears. "So they're just going to keep on getting sick and dying?"

Jamie nodded. There was no missing the catch in his voice as he continued. "If it's anything like the other tribes, they could lose half their people before it's over."

"Half?" I looked around the circle in alarm. Half of these big-hearted men would be dead? How could something like that happen? And if they didn't die, they'd all be hit with the heartache of losing friends and loved ones! All from a disease that could be cured?! I felt myself getting mad. "You gotta do something, Jamie!"

"Like what?" he asked.

"I don't know. Like . . . like . . . " I was getting more and more upset, but I couldn't think of anything.

Suddenly we were interrupted by someone passing us a wooden bowl of milk. Only it didn't exactly look like milk. Come to think of it, it didn't smell like it either. All the dried fish had made me pretty thirsty, but I wasn't sure if drinking this was such a good idea. Jamie agreed.

"You might want to pass on that, Wally."

"What is it?"

"Beer—made of manioc . . . and human spit."

Suddenly, I struggled to keep my dinner down as I passed the bowl on to Jamie.

"And they wonder how diseases spread," Jamie said as he stared sadly into the bowl.

"You really want to help these people, don't you?" I asked.

"Don't you?" Jamie looked up to me.

Before I could answer there was a commotion at the far end of the hut. A bunch of men were dancing and jumping around.

"What's that?" I asked.

"You don't want to know."

"Tell me."

"They're smoking drugs. They're hallucinating and asking the demons to come and take control of their bodies."

"You're kidding me!" I exclaimed.

The look in Jamie's eyes said he wasn't.

"But that's, that's like witchcraft." I stuttered.

Jamie nodded, even sadder than before.

I watched as another man began leaping and jumping and acting out of control. Only the problem was . . . he wasn't acting.

Suddenly our circle began to clap and cheer. I looked over to the doorway and was happy to see George come back into the hut. I'd been kinda missing him. At first he looked more naked than usual until I realized it was because he didn't have his monkey on his shoulder.

I caught his eye and gave him a grin as he handed a wooden platter of meat to the men. He tried to return the smile, but he didn't have much luck at it. I motioned for him to sit beside me, but he just turned and walked out.

"What's with him?" I asked.

Jamie looked more miserable than ever.

"Is he okay?"

Jamie shook his head. "The people believe that to keep the spirits happy you have to make sacrifices to them."

"Sacrifices? Like what?"

Jamie hesitated.

"Like what, Jamie?"

"Animals." He took a deep breath. "The greater the spirit, the greater the sacrifice."

"But what's that got to do with George being so sad?"

Again Jamie hesitated.

"Jamie?"

Finally he spoke. "Did you see his monkey when he came back in?"

"No, but what's that got to—" And then it hit me. "No way!"

Jamie didn't answer.

"Not his pet monkey!?" I practically shouted. "They wouldn't make him kill his pet monkey!"

"What do you think is on that platter they're passing?"

I looked to the platter as it slowly approached us. My stomach began to turn. My head began to get light. I wasn't sure if I was going to get sick, or pass out, or both. I rose unsteadily to my feet.

"Wally, you okay?"

"Yeah . . . I just . . . I gotta go outside."

I knew the men were staring at me, but I had to get out of there. I had to get away from that platter. I had to get away from everybody. I wanted to shout at them. To scream and yell. I wanted to hit them. I wanted to do all those things. But by the time I staggered out of the hut and into the rain, all I could do was cry.

I don't know how long I was there, but finally I heard Jamie's voice. "You okay?"

"No! I'm not okay! Everything's awful! Everything's ugly! Stupid!"

Jamie nodded. "Everything but the people."

I was furious, but I didn't know at whom. I tried to say something but only managed to squeeze out a little sob.

Jamie said nothing. After a moment I felt his hand on my shoulder. "Now you know why we're here," he said softly. "Now you know why we're trying to help."

"But the pain," I croaked. "These people are dying, they're killing themselves, they're, they're . . . How do you handle all this?"

Jamie took a deep breath. I could tell he was fighting back his own feelings. Finally he answered. "You live with it, Wally. You live with it, and you try to make it go away by doing what you can."

Chapter 7
Farewells

Since they didn't have beds in the hut, everyone slept in one of those hammock thingies. Mine was pretty comfortable once I got into it. But getting into it was the trick. It seems every time I hopped into one side, I'd go flying out the other.

Hop.

FLIIINGGGG . . .

"WHOOOAAAAA!"

KER-THUMP! (The *KER-THUMP* was me hitting the ground.)

"They're supposed to be beds," Jamie chuckled, glancing over to me as I lay flat on my back. "Not slingshots."

"I know that," I scowled as I got up and tried to hop back in. "It's just gonna take a little time to get the hang of—"

Hop.

FLIIINGGGG . . .
"WHOOOAAAAA!"
KER-THUMP!
"Then again, maybe I'll just spend the night here on the ground."

Of course all the men in the hut laughed, and of course, I gave them my world famous Wally-McDoogle-the-Idiot-grin. It felt kinda good doing what I did best, being the source of everyone's laughter. And for a moment I almost forgot all our problems . . . almost, but not quite . . .

Twenty minutes later I was safe and secure in the hammock (thanks to the guys tying me in it like a mummy)—but I still couldn't sleep. I was faced with a major decision . . . what to worry about the most:

A. Being lost in the rain forest.
B. Being chased by angry poachers.
C. Being with these people who are sick and dying.
D. Worrying about Dad worrying and calling up Mom so she'll worry even more.
E. All of the above.

Not wanting to miss out, I checked letter "E." This meant my mind raced around and around. And when it got tired of racing around and around, it started racing back and forth. Then it started going up and down. In short, my brain was getting a lot of exercise. Too much. I had to think of something to help it rest. Finally I had it. My "Techno Boy" story. True, I didn't have ol' Betsy with me to write anything down, but I still had my mind . . . and my not-so-normal imagination . . .

When we last left Techno Boy, he was being sucked into the belly of a giant flying saucer with the rest of the people from Earth. It is the worst of all worsts. Well, actually the third worst of all worsts. The worst of all worsts is discovering you're having creamed spinach for dinner—while the second worst of all worsts is having to listen to the stupid jokes fellow earthlings tell as they're being sucked into flying saucers.

"Hey, Techno Boy!" It's Mrs. Sludge, his English teacher. She's rising off the ground just a few feet away and asking, "What's the difference between an elephant and a matter baby?"

"I don't know," our hero sighs, "what's a matter baby?"

"Got me, what's a matter with you, baby? Har-Har-Har."

Techno can stand no more. Quickly he tugs on his thumb. But this is no ordinary thumb. As he pulls it, his thumb grows longer and longer until we discover it is a giant radio antenna specifically tuned to the frequencies of all power lawn mowers.

What? You didn't know lawn mowers reacted to radio waves? Haven't you ever wondered why, whenever you tune into the radio or start watching a good TV show, your mom suddenly decides it's time for you to quit lying around the house and go mow the lawn? (See how educational these stories can be?)

Now where was I? Oh yeah . . .

Our superhero presses four tiny freckles on his arm. Now, to the untrained eye, they look like freckles, but by now we all know better than that, don't we? They're not freckles, they're special, remote-control buttons.

Immediately mowers all over the country start up their engines. But our hero is not thinking of mowing the nation's lawns (although he could stand a little extra cash over the summer). Instead, he turns his left ear to the right and his right ear to the left. (Don't try this at home, kids, unless you're a Transformer Toy.) This, of course, revs up all the mower engines faster than a used car salesman's mouth. They begin to take off . . . literally. Like helicopters, millions of lawn mowers lift out of their garages and soar high into the sky.

"What are you doing, Techno Boy?" a voice from inside the flying saucer shouts. "Resistance is futile. Quit now."

The lawn mowers arrive. Techno Boy leaps on the nearest riding mower (a Torro, of course) and shouts for his fellow prisoners to do likewise. But they are too busy cracking jokes to hear.

"Hey, Techno Boy," Ms. Lottahype calls. "What's black and white and black and white and black and white?"

"Please, Ms. Lottahype, just take hold of that mower over there and—"

"A zebra rolling down a hill!" She doubles over in laughter.

"Everyone!" Techno Boy cries, "You
must grab hold of these lawn mowers.
They've got enough power to pull you out
of the tractor beam and fre—"

But it does no good. Everyone is too
busy yelling jokes and shouting punch
lines.

"What would happen if every car in the
nation turned pink?" someone cries.

"You'd have a pink carnation!" another
shouts.

"Where does an 800-pound gorilla sit?"
somebody yells.

"Anywhere he wants!" another answers.

Techno Boy is beside himself. What can
he do? The lawn mowers are all hover-
ing, waiting to help these poor people,
but no one will take hold of them.

Suddenly our heroically handsome hunk
of junk has an idea. Techno Boy throws
his trusty Torro into "We-Better-Try-
Something-Else-And-We-Better-Try-It-
Fast." He and all the other lawn mowers roar away.

"Where's he going?" someone shouts.

"He's deserting us!" somebody screams.

"Why'd the chicken cross the street?"
another cries.

However, Techno Boy is no longer there
to hear. He's gone.

But not for long. (After all, he is
our hero and heroes are expected to
save the day.) Soon there is a low
droning on the horizon. Closer and
closer it comes. Louder and louder it
drones.

Suddenly the lawn mowers come into view.
Only now there are strange boxes dangling
from each of their handlebars . . .

Could it be? Great Scott, yes! They're
TV sets. Big ones, small ones, miniature ones, color ones, old black and
white ones. And they are all heading
directly toward the people.

What can it be? What clever trick is
our rechargeable hero planning to pull
off with all these TVs?

* * * * *

We were awake early the next morning. As soon
as they untied me from my hammock I leaped out
and hit the ground . . .
FLIIINGGGG . . .
"WHOOOAAAAA!"
KER-THUMP!

I tell you this *"Flinging"* . . . *"Whoaing"* and *"Ker-Thumping"* was getting to be kinda old.

It had stopped raining outside, and the ground was covered with dew. Well, we call it dew. George and his buddies called it "star spit." (Kinda makes you glad to sleep inside at night, doesn't it?)

"You must leave now," the shaman said, "before the spirits waken and make you sick."

Once again Jamie tried to talk the men into coming to the medical clinic to get inoculated from the disease. And once again they had the same answer as before. "Thanks, but no thanks."

After some more dried fish and manioc root (not to be mistaken for orange juice and an Egg McMuffin) we started to head back to the waterfall with George. It wasn't easy saying good-bye to these people. We'd only known them a few hours, but they already seemed like old friends. As we left, the shaman put a necklace of bones and teeth around each of our necks. I wasn't crazy about the idea—I mean *whose* bones and teeth were they, anyway? But I could tell the guy was doing it to be friendly so I kept quiet. I did a lot of squirming, but it was quiet squirming.

When we reached the edge of the clearing, we turned back to the village one last time. I'll never forget what I saw. It's like a picture in my brain. The whole tribe was huddled together. They had all come out to wish Jamie and me, two total strangers, a safe journey. Talk about a loving people. I tried to swallow back the lump I felt growing in my throat. I knew Jamie was doing the same. They were good people. Very good.

We turned back to the forest, and a dozen steps later the village behind us had completely disappeared. With all the vines and trees it was like it never existed.

"You saw a real neat thing," Jamie said as we followed George along the path. "They won't be around much longer."

"How's that?" I asked.

"Four hundred years ago there were over four million pure Indians around here. In a few years, there'll be less than 100,000."

I gave a low whistle. "Where do they all go?"

"Some are dying of disease, others are moving away to the cities."

"Well, at least there they'll have TV." I grinned, throwing in some of my famous McDoogle humor.

"Yeah," Jamie said, "along with more disease, more poverty, and more mistreatment."

So much for humor.

Jamie continued. There was no missing the sadness creeping in his voice. "That's another reason we're trying to reach people like this—to help them beat all the junk the world's throwing at them."

I nodded silently. This missionary stuff was beginning to sound a lot more important than I'd thought. Jamie really cared for them, and now I could see why. In fact, when we stopped for lunch (manioc and dried stingray—yum, yum) I wasn't surprised to hear him trying to tell George about God. At first I was kind of embarrassed. Don't ask me why, but that's how I get when you talk about Jesus and stuff. But not Jamie.

He picked up a stick and started to draw in the dirt. He spoke mostly English, but with the help of the drawings, George seemed to understand.

"This is God over here," he said as he drew a little stick figure.

"And this is us over here." He drew another figure:

"Now between us and God, there is this big canyon, this big gap called 'sin.' Sin is like all the wrong we've ever done."

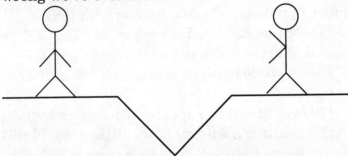

George nodded. He seemed to really be getting into it.

Jamie kept going. "Here we are, on one side totally cut off from God by this big canyon. So how can we ever cross over it?"

George looked up anxiously for the answer.

"Well, that's where Jesus comes in. You see Jesus came down from heaven and died." Jamie drew a picture of a cross in the chasm:

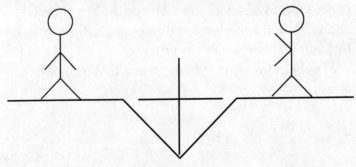

"Jesus?" George asked, pointing at the cross.

"That's right; 'Jesus,'" Jamie said. "Jesus took the punishment we deserve. So now you and I can cross that canyon and be friends with God."

George looked up, his eyes wide. "Jesus?" he asked, jabbing his finger at the cross again.

Jamie nodded. "Jesus came so we can be friends with God."

"*Jesus?*" George repeated in astonishment, again pointing his finger at the little cross. "Jesus . . . make us friends?" Now he was pointing to the drawing of God.

"That's right—Jesus gave His life so we can be friends with God. He gave His life to save ours."

George continued to stare. Jamie and I traded looks. We weren't sure what was going to happen next, but neither of us were breathing.

Finally, Jamie spoke. "Would you like that? Would you like to be friends with God?"

Then suddenly, out of the blue, George stood up, snorted, and headed down the path. We glanced to each other. Jamie looked disappointed. I guess he figured George wasn't buying it.

Maybe he was, maybe he wasn't. We'd soon find out . . . .

Chapter 8

Reunion with Some Old Buddies

An hour later we arrived at the waterfall. Funny, it didn't seem as frightening from the bottom looking up as it did from the top falling down.

George came to a stop and motioned to a steep, rocky path beside the waterfall. Obviously this was the route we were supposed to take. It didn't look too bad . . . if you happened to be a mountain goat or had a spare helicopter. But if you happened to be a professional klutz, it looked like there could be a lot of pain involved.

"I hope somebody brought the Tylenol," I said as I checked the "softness" of the ground where we were standing—the ground my body would soon be hitting from the trail above.

Jamie barely heard. He was too busy saying good-bye to George. I could tell things were getting pretty emotional as they kept hugging and promising to see each other again.

Then it was my turn. I wanted to say so much. You know, little things like, "Thanks for saving my life." I also wanted to say how sorry I was about his monkey, or how I'd love to be pen pals if he'd just give me his village's ZIP code. But when we hugged nothing came out. Nothing but a hoarse kind of . . . "Thanks."

He nodded and stepped back. Then, before I could make any more great, profound statements, he turned and started toward the forest.

"Let's go, Wally!"

I looked up. Jamie was already halfway up the side of the waterfall. I looked back to George. He continued toward the forest, blending more and more into the trees.

With a heavy sigh, I turned and started up the rocks—not, of course, without the usual slips,

WHOA . . .

Slides—

OOOPPS . . .

and . . .

KER-THUMPS . . .

I got up, brushed off the mud, and started again. And failed again.

And started again.

And failed again.

"Quit horsing around," Jamie shouted. By now he had reached the top where he could sit and watch the whole show. He tried not to laugh, but he was about as successful with that as I was with my climbing.

"I'm not horsing around," I shouted as I slipped—*WHOA* . . . and fell—*KER-THUMP* . . . back on the ground again.

I glanced back at George. He had stopped to watch my performance and was also trying not to laugh. (Isn't it great to know you can bring so much joy into the world?)

"Don't they have P.E. or athletics in your school?" Jamie shouted down to me.

"Sure," I groaned as I rose to my feet and counted how many bones I'd broken on that last fall. "But the closest I come to taking part in athletics is pushing the channel selector on the TV remote."

I tried a few more times, and finally, through sheer luck (or maybe I'd just run out of bones to break) I made it to the top. I took one last look back toward George, but he was nowhere in sight. He had already gone.

"See you around," I said softly . . . "and thanks." Then I turned back to look at Jamie. But Jamie was gone now, too.

"Jamie . . ." I called, stumbling to my feet and starting down the trail. "Jamie, wait up. Jamie, where are YOOOOOUUUUU? . . ."

Suddenly the path under my feet moved. Well, it really didn't move, it just sort of disappeared . . . which just sort of sent me falling and tumbling . . . into this sort of a deep, dark, bottomless pit!

I wanted to shout, to scream, to cry for help. Unfortunately the only thing I managed to squeeze out was a rather pathetic:

"Uh-oh . . ."

*   *   *   *   *

I don't remember hitting the ground. I don't even remember being pulled out of the pit. What I do remember was waking up and noticing the sky was where the ground should be, and the ground was where the sky should be. I also noticed I was moving without walking and that my wrists and feet were strapped together. At last I figured it out. I was being carried upside down with my feet and arms tied to a long pole.

"Glad you could join us." It was Jamie's voice.

I craned my neck and saw him beside me. He was also upside down and on a pole.

"Is this a dream?" I asked. "'Cause if it is, I'd like to wake up now."

"You kids shut up!"

The voice came from behind. Its ugly meanness sounded strangely familiar. I looked back to see a man who was carrying our poles on each of his shoulders. This was no dream. It was a nightmare. He was the big poacher whose face I'd sneezed into.

I looked forward to see who was carrying our poles up ahead. He was also an old friend—the one with the big scar across his face.

"Now that we nabbed them, I say we throw them to the crocs and be done with it," the big guy grumbled. "Everyone will think it's an accident and in a few days we can get back to work."

Now you don't have to be a rocket scientist to figure by "crocs" he meant crocodiles.

"What if they should get away?" the guy with the scar argued.

"Nobody gets away from an Amazon crocodile— 'specially not punks like these."

Boy, do I know how to call 'em or what? It *was* crocodiles. Normally I'd be pretty proud over being so right, but at the moment I had a few other emotions to experience . . . like, raw, overwhelming fear!

"You guys can't kill us!" I screamed.

"Why not?" Scar Face demanded.

"'Cause . . . 'cause . . . well, because." I knew my logic was a little weak, but it was the best I could come up with on such short notice.

"Yeah, well it ain't our decision anyway," Big Guy growled. "Hector's getting back from the doctor tomorrow. He'll tell us what to do."

"Who's Hector?" Jamie demanded.

With any luck Hector would be some grandfatherly type boss who would look upon us with compassion—who would see us as sweet, innocent kids who'd never hurt a soul.

"Hector's the guy whose leg you broke when you knocked him down in the cave." Big Guy said.

"Oh, that Hector . . ." I swallowed nervously. "Well, I hope he's the forgiving type."

"Oh, he's forgiving," Big Guy chuckled. "Just ask my partner, there."

"Yeah, he's forgiving," Scar Face agreed, "I got me this cut across my face to prove it."

Both men laughed.

"I don't get it," Jamie asked. "What's that scar got to do with his forgiveness?"

"Hector gave it to me for accidentally knockin' over his coffee one morning." He laughed louder. Big Guy joined in. Pretty soon they were both yucking it up real good.

Now, don't get me wrong. I like a good joke as much as the next guy. I would have joined in the laughter, too, but it's kind of hard to laugh when you're busy trying not to cry.

Chapter 9

McDoogle Munchies

It was night when we finally arrived at their camp—if you call a sheet of plastic hanging between some trees and two hammocks strung under it a "camp." We were near the river and cave where we first ran into these not-so-nice-guys. Hector was still off at the doctor's and wouldn't be back till morning. What luck. That meant we could live at least another whole night. Oh, boy!

But instead of enjoying our good fortune by sitting around the campfire toasting marshmallows and singing songs, Big Guy and Scar Face had other ideas. Like tying us to a tree just a few yards from the river. Like drinking a whole flask of whisky and staggering toward their hammocks to sleep.

"Hey, what about us?" Jamie whined. He wasn't complaining about the whisky. He was complaining about how they got nice cozy hammocks for beds and we got nice soggy mud. Jamie had a point. I don't know about you, but I always like to have a good night's sleep before I die in the morning.

"What're you bellyaching about now?" Scar Face grumbled as he finished off the booze and climbed clumsily into his hammock.

"You just can't leave us here on the ground," Jamie cried. "Not this close to the river."

"Why not?"

"What about the snakes?" Jamie demanded. His voice shook and it had nothing to do with being cold. "What about the spiders . . . what about the crocs?"

"It'll just save us the trouble," Big Guy mumbled from his hammock. The whisky was having its effect, and he was already drifting off to sleep.

"Yeah," Scar Face belched, "so keep yer yaps shut, or we'll (another belch) put an end to you right here and now."

Well, okay, if he wanted to be that way about it . . . .

A few minutes later both men were snoring like chain saws.

Jamie and I tried our best to squirm out of the knots. No luck. Next we tried to rub up and down against the tree—you know, to wear out the ropes like they do on TV. I guess TV stars use different rope, 'cause all we succeeded in doing was wearing out our skin.

Then I heard it. It was very soft. But there was no mistaking the faint sound of water splashing. Someone or some*thing* was getting out of the river.

"Jamie," I whispered, "Jamie, you hear that?"

"Yeah . . ." he whispered back.

"What is it?"

"I don't think you want to know."

He was right. But if you're dying you should probably know some of the details—the little things like how it's happening . . . just in case there are forms and stuff to fill out when you get to heaven.

Next came the rustling of grass. It was getting closer by the second. I stared into the darkness but couldn't see a thing.

I turned my head toward Jamie. "Tell me it's not a crocodile."

"Okay," he said, "it's not a crocodile."

I hesitated. Somehow he didn't sound so convincing.

"Are you telling the truth?"

"No," he said.

"So it is a crocodile?"

"I'm not supposed to tell you."

"Jamie! What do we do?"

"Just keep still," he whispered. "Crocs usually don't kill on land."

I sighed in relief. "They don't?"

"No, they drag their prey into the water, *then* they kill them."

So much for relief. I couldn't believe my luck. Here I had traveled thousands of miles, made friends with a remote tribe of Indians, finally understood why we need missionaries—and for what? To become late-night junk food for some crocodile with a bad case of the munchies?

By now the rustling grass sounded like it was right beside me. And for good reason. It *WAS* right beside me!

Jamie whispered so softly I could barely hear. "Don't move a muscle."

No problem. I couldn't move if I wanted to.

Suddenly the sound stopped. That was the good news. The bad news was I started to feel soft, cool breath on my arm. I couldn't believe it! The thing was sniffing me! Suddenly I remembered it'd been a couple of days since my last shower. I hoped he didn't mind. Then again, maybe it would be better if he *did* mind.

He stayed at my side all night . . . or maybe it was just a couple of seconds (it's kind of hard to keep track during times like that). All sorts of thoughts raced through my head. Did Opera, my buddy back home, remember he could have my CD collection? Did Mom and Dad have my life insurance paid up? Would dividing compound fractions be any easier in heaven?

The breath slowly moved up my arm to my shoulder, then to my neck. Oh, great! The thing was starting to sniff my face! Talk about a case of bad breath. I don't want to complain, but it was enough to kill a cow . . . or a wanna-be writer with Woody Allen glasses who happened to be tied to a tree by poachers.

I couldn't help myself. I had to look. Slowly, I moved my head. And there we were, eyeball to eyeglasses . . . the crocodile and me. It was like staring at a giant pair of alligator skin shoes . . . without the shoes.

First, I noticed his nose. His nostrils kept flaring in and out as they gave me a careful once over. I looked down his long, pebbly nose (talk about a bad case of acne!). Then I saw his eyes. Their slits were wide open but looked completely lifeless. Then I saw the teeth. Ah, yes, the teeth. We're talking major overbite. I don't want to be rude, but this guy could keep a crew of orthodontists in Mercedes for the rest of their lives!

I couldn't wait any longer. The time had come. Those of you who know me, know what I had to do. I opened my mouth and did what I do best:

AUGHHHHHHHHH!

Ol' crocy boy pulled back in a start, then he opened his mouth and shouted back:

ROOOOOOOOOOAAAAAAARRRR!

I was shocked. I expected a hiss or a bark or something. Anything but a roar. Still, for not being a lion, he did a pretty good job.

I looked directly into his mouth. I saw nothing but teeth and tongue and more teeth and even more teeth. I tell you, if that was going to be home for the rest of my life, it was definitely going to be a bit on the cramped side.

AUGHHHHHHHHHHHHHHHHHHHHHHH! I screamed back.

"*ROOOOOOOOOAAAAAAAAAAAAARRRRRRRR RRRR!*" he roared back.

So he thinks he can outpanic me, does he. . . .

AUGHHHHHHHHHHHHHHHHHHHHHHHHHHHH HHHHHHHHHHHHHHHHHH!

ROOOOOOOOOOOAAAAA— squeal, squeal, cough, cough."

Suddenly his head thrashed to the side. I was a little confused. Then I saw George. He was kneeling right over the critter! The rest happened so fast I'm still not sure I saw it all. . . .

Somehow George hopped on the croc's back. But he wasn't going for a ride, he was trying to flip it over. The crocodile gnashed his teeth and whipped his powerful tail while George did his best to avoid both. There was also a lot of shouting and hysterical screaming. Most of it mine.

Scar Face and Big Guy leaped out of their hammocks, and staggered around in the dark doing their own version of shouting and screaming. They were so drunk they didn't know where they were, let alone what was happening.

Meanwhile, back at the wrestling match, there suddenly seemed to be a lot of blood. Unfortunately, it didn't all look like crocodile blood. At last George managed to flip the creature onto its back. I noticed the glint of steel in his hand—obviously a knife. But the croc was in no mood to be a Thanksgiving turkey. He dug his tail into the ground and flipped them both over. Now the animal was on top of George!

"GEORGE!!!" I screamed. *"George! George!!"* I knew my screaming wasn't that helpful, but it was all I could offer at the time.

But George didn't need any of my help. Once again he managed to flip the animal over. Once again there was more thrashing and snarling. Then suddenly everything stopped. Just like that. One minute growling, thrashing, snarling—the next, total silence . . . except for George's heavy breathing.

The croc was dead. George had saved our lives. Well, not yet . . .

"Get him!" Big Guy bellowed as he lunged for George.

"Watch it!" I yelled.

George looked up and leaped away just in time. Big Guy, who was having a little problem sobering up, stumbled over the dead crocodile. Then, thanks to some fancy kicking by George, Big Guy tumbled head over heels, down the bank, and into the river.

Ker-Splash!

"Help me!" he screamed (along with lots of other colorful language). "Help me, help me!"

Quickly George reached out and cut the ropes that tied our hands. I noticed his arm was pretty chewed up. But that was nothing compared to his leg. It was your basic hamburger. He may have killed the croc, but the croc definitely left him a little something to be remembered by.

Suddenly Scar Face was towering over us. He looked kind of confused—like he didn't know whether he should kill us or help his screaming partner (who was doing a pretty good imitation of drowning).

We didn't wait for him to make up his mind.

"That way!" Jamie shouted.

We took off—away from the river and toward the caves.

Scar Face screamed and swore at us. I'll have to give you the Christian translation:

"I'm so sorry you boys have to rush off. Say, I have a splendid idea, as soon as I assist my colleague we shall pursue you and perhaps try to do you great bodily harm!"

As we raced through the forest, we could tell George was having a hard time with his leg. Jamie and I grabbed him on both sides and helped him hobble along.

We made okay time, but not as okay as Scar Face and Big Guy. As soon as Scar Face dragged his buddy out of the water, they began chasing us. Now they were closing in fast.

"This way!" Jamie yelled as we veered sharply to the right. I had to take his word for it because it was too dark to see much of anything.

And then it happened:

SNAP . . . zing.

Immediately Jamie pulled us down into the bushes.

"What was that?" I whispered.

"What do you think it was?" Jamie whispered back. "It's a rifle!"

I'd always thought rifles were supposed to go *K-BAMB*, but I guess that's just on TV. I did, however, recognize the *zing*. That was definitely a bullet sailing over our heads.

"I don't think they're trying to shoot us," Jamie whispered, "just scare us."

"Well, they're doing a pretty good job." I shuddered.

"Just stay still."

We froze in the undergrowth, and a few seconds later the men raced by. They were so close, we could have reached out and touched them. We didn't. And they didn't see us. But as they ran past, Scar Face fired a couple more rounds into the dark.

SNAP . . . SNAP

Fortunately there were no more *zings* over our heads.

Once they'd passed, Jamie cautiously rose to his feet and whispered, "Come on!"

But George had other ideas. He whispered something. Jamie whispered back. Pretty soon they got into a big argument. I didn't understand it all. The best I could make out was that George wanted to act as a decoy. He wanted to draw the men's attention to him, so Jamie and I could make a clean get-away.

"That's crazy!" Jamie argued. "If they catch you, there's no telling what they'll do."

George shook his head and repeated his plan.

"No way," Jamie insisted. "You're not going to risk your life to save ours."

Without a word George grabbed a stick and scratched something into the dirt.

"What is it?" I asked.

"It's . . ." Jamie squinted through the dark. "It's a cross."

George nodded his head enthusiastically.

"I don't get it." I whispered.

"Jesus," George whispered tapping his stick at the cross. "Jesus."

Jamie and I exchanged looks, neither one of us understanding.

George grabbed his stick and drew a bigger cross. "Jesus," he insisted. "Jesus, Jesus."

Our response was the same—blank stares.

Suddenly the men's voices grew louder. I guess they realized we'd quit running and were hiding, so now they were doubling back to find us.

"What do we do?" I whispered.

"Just stay low and be still," Jamie answered.

The men's voices grew louder.

And then, when they were nearly on top of us, George leaped to his feet, let out a loud "WHOOP!" and took off limping through the brush.

"There they are!" Big Guy shouted. Scar Face raised his rifle and fired off another round.

SNAP!

And another . . .

SNAP!

But George just kept on running. He just kept whooping it up, making as much noise as he could, while dashing through the forest.

The men took off after him, cursing all the way.

I started to stand, but Jamie quickly pulled me down. I looked at him. He shook his head. He didn't have to say another word. I knew what he was thinking. This was George's choice . . . this is what he wanted to do. There was nothing we could do to stop him . . . and, at the moment, there was nothing we could do to help him.

There were more rifle shots as the men's voices started to fade into the night. Only God knew if they'd catch George . . . or what they'd do to him if they did. And since only God knew, I fired off a little prayer asking Him to help.

After several minutes, Jamie and I slowly rose to our feet. The yelling was much farther off. George was obviously giving them a run for their money. We hoped it would last. But with his wounded leg, we both had our doubts.

We had said good-bye to George twice that day. And this second good-bye was a lot more painful than the first. Neither Jamie nor I could look at each other. It had something to do with the tears that were trying to fill our eyes.

Without a word, we turned and silently headed for home.

Chapter 10

Wrapping Up

Of course, everyone made a big deal when we got back to Jamie's house. His mother, Doctor Mom, checked us out so many times I got to feeling guilty that there wasn't anything wrong with me. Dad and everyone kept asking a zillion questions, and we kept telling the story over and over again. I don't know 'bout Jamie, but each time I told it, I was doing a lot less screaming and a lot more saving the day.

Normally it would have been neat having everyone make such a fuss over us, but both Jamie and I had something else on our minds . . .

George.

Was he all right? Did Big Guy and Scar Face catch him? Did he make it back to his village? But more importantly, we kept wondering why he did what he did. Why did he risk his life to save ours?

And what did he mean by drawing the cross in the dirt and saying "Jesus" over and over again?

It wasn't until the following night when we were both in bed that Jamie suddenly cried out, "I've got it!"

"I hope it's not contagious," I mumbled as I turned over trying to get back to sleep.

"No, Wally, listen up. I know what George meant. I know what he was trying to say!"

My eyes popped open, and I sat up.

"He was saying he was going to do what Jesus did!"

"What?" I asked.

"Remember when I kept drawing the cross in the dirt . . . remember how I kept saying Jesus gave up his life to save ours?"

"Well, yeah, but—"

"Don't you get it!? George *did* understand what we were saying about Jesus. In fact, he was telling us he was going to do the same thing . . . he was going to risk his life to save ours."

"Wow . . ." I exclaimed as I slowly thought it through. "So you think he like believed what you said about Jesus—you think maybe he became a Christian?"

"I don't know." Jamie sighed. "But I know he understood the idea . . . and I know he believed it enough to imitate it by saving us!"

I could only shake my head at the thought. "That is so cool. . . ."

Sleep didn't come easy after that. Maybe George hadn't become an "official" Christian. (Then again maybe he had.) But at least he understood and believed in Jesus enough to show His type of love for us.

It was amazing. In one short night George had shown more of God's love to us than I had shown in my entire life. Granted, he may not have had my sparkling Sunday school attendance record, or memorized as many Bible verses . . . but when he stood before God, I had a sneaking suspicion he was going to be all right.

It was one of the warmest feelings I'd ever had. To be part of telling someone about Jesus. Like I said, I was no Billy Graham and I doubted if I'd be signing up as a missionary right away. But I finally understood why missionaries do what they do. I finally understood how they could get so excited about their work.

I finally understood their love.

*   *   *   *   *

Two days later we were all packed up and hiking back to the landing strip. Lots of other guys had arrived to continue building the medical clinic, but Dad had to get home and back to his job.

As the plane pulled up and opened its door, Jamie and I said some pretty emotional good-byes.

Of course we made the usual promises to write, and of course we knew we wouldn't. But that was okay. We also knew we wouldn't forget each other, either. No way.

I stood on the wing of the plane and took one last look around. It had started to rain again. But the villagers had come out anyway. They were waving and grinning. And right then and there, I knew I'd be back. Maybe not to this exact village or to these exact people. But probably to another people, another place. Maybe for only a week to help out like Dad . . . but I'd be back.

"Let's go!" Dad shouted from inside the plane.

I turned and ducked my head down, but not enough. I hit it hard against the roof. Of course everyone laughed, and of course I grinned. It was nice to get back into the swing of things.

More good-byes and waves as we taxied past the cows and revved up the engines to take off. I watched out the window as we picked up speed. And then I saw it: a group of men coming out of the jungle. I craned my neck for a better look, but I lost them behind a bunch of huts.

By the time they came back into view, we were higher and I could see them better. They were an Indian tribe! You could tell by their clothes (or lack of them).

I asked if we could land again, but the pilot was on a tight schedule and didn't have any extra fuel. Still, he agreed to circle the village so I could get a longer look.

It was a small group of men, about ten or twelve. They were carrying a couple of guys tied upside down on poles (one of my least favorite ways to travel). The two guys were white, with Western clothes and . . .

Hold it! Could it be? I pressed flat against the window for a better look . . . YES! It was them! Big Guy and Scar Face!

And leading the group . . . I pressed harder against the window . . . and leading the group was the shaman. Beside him was some kid. Some kid with a bad limp. Some kid that could only be . . . George!

I banged on the window. "George! George!" But of course, he couldn't hear me. Just as well. If he saw me in the plane, he'd probably worry that I'd been eaten by a big, metal bird.

And then, just like that, the trees blocked my view.

But that was okay. I had seen all I needed to see.

George was all right. The bad guys were caught. Not only that, but by bringing them into the village, the shaman would be exposed to the new medical clinic.

Maybe Jamie's folks could talk him into taking some of their medicine back to his tribe. Maybe his people wouldn't have to keep on dying. Maybe someone might even tell them more about God.

I reached up and fingered the necklace around my neck. The one the shaman had given me. I still wasn't crazy about the bones and teeth, but I knew it would always remind me of these people and others like them. And it would always remind me of their needs.

An hour later I was getting a little bored. I mean if you've seen one jungle, you've seen them all, right?

I reached down and pulled out ol' Betsy. She'd grown a little dusty over the week, but when I opened her lid and snapped her on, her screen glowed just as brightly as ever. With all the extra time on my hands, I figured I'd better find out how Techno Boy was doing . . . .

When we last left our microchip marvel, the entire world was paralyzed by a comedy beam. Every citizen was telling terrible jokes. All this as they were being sucked into alien flying saucers.

Having tied TV sets to every lawn mower in the country (which were flying around like miniature helicopters), our gorgeous good guy quickly positions the screens so every citizen of the world can see one.

But before he can reveal his perfect plan, the flying saucers start firing wads of pre-chewed Trident sugarless gum (the preferred gum of space monsters everywhere). No one's sure where they developed the taste for the gum, but they really go for the "sugarless" since it helps keep their twenty-three layers of fangs cavity-free.

Soon our hero is covered in gum. I mean, *really* covered. Worse than underneath the lunch table in the cafeteria.

"Somebody . . ." he cries, "somebody, help me!"

Immediately he is surrounded by volunteers. They want desperately to help, but all they can do is tell jokes.

"Say, Techno Boy," one of them cries.

"What's the last thing to go through a grasshopper's mind when he hits the windshield?"

"I don't know," Techno Boy groans.

"His tail!" comes the answer.

"Please . . ." our hero's voice grows weaker and weaker. It's obvious the gum is clogging up his gears.

The crowd wants to help but can't. "Say," somebody shouts, "what's the difference between a cow's tail and a water pump handle?"

"I . . . don't . . . know . . ."

"Then I'll never send you for water . . . har-har-har."

Finally, using his last ounce of energy, Techno Boy reaches for the switch inside his nose. A secret switch. A switch he never likes using, but it's getting toward the end of the story so he better do something. He hates to do what he has to do. But he has to do it, so he does it . . .

He flips the switch and suddenly all the TV screens flicker. Next an old "Gilligan's Island" rerun pops up on all their sets.

"Don't you see," Techno Boy gasps, "if you leave . . . if you allow yourself to be taken by these spaceships, you'll never know if Gilligan and Mary Ann ever get off the island."

There's a brief murmur of concern.

Techno Boy flips to another channel. It's a "Cosby" rerun. "If you leave, you'll never know if Bill and his wife ever get all the kids out of the house."

These deep questions cause everyone to grow more and more serious—and, as they grow more serious, the power of the comedy beam loses its strength. Gradually, the people start drifting back toward the ground.

"Stop it!" the speakers on the flying saucers blare. "Stop it at once!" Desperately, they crank up the comedy beam even stronger.

Giggles begin to return to the crowd. Someone yells, "What does an 800-pound canary sing?"

"No!" others cry, "We must not give in! We can fight their comedy, we can resist the temptation! Please, Techno Boy," they cry, "keep asking us those deep questions, keep making us think!"

Techno Boy flips to another show.
"What about this guy here on 'Home Im-
provement?' . . . will he ever build
something that doesn't fall apart?"

The crowd grows even more serious . . .
the beam loses more control over them.

Now it's time to ask the most serious
question of all. One that will break the
comedy beam's power for good. He flips
to the closing credits of "The Brady
Bunch." "And what about these poor
kids?" he shouts.

Everyone gasps. They'd completely
forgotten about Marsha and the gang.

"Will they ever break out of these
little boxes at the end of each show?
Will they ever stop singing that song?"

That does it. You just don't bring up
a serious subject like "The Brady Bunch"
and not expect some response. The power
of the comedy beam is broken. The people
tumble back to the ground.

A frustrated and beaten squadron of
spaceships close their hatches and pre-
pare to leave. But not before broadcast-
ing their final message. "You haven't
seen the last of us, Techno Boy." They

seem to hesitate a moment, then continue, "Listen, about Gilligan and Mary Ann. . . will they ever get off that island?"

But Techno Boy doesn't answer. He is surrounded by the grateful population of Earth. They crowd around him with thousands of butter knives in an effort to pry off all the wads of chewing gum.

And for good reason.

Who knows when he will be needed next? Who knows what dark and sinister plan is already being hatched to endanger the planet? But fear not, gentle earthlings. For wherever danger lurks, there Techno Boy will be, chugging motor oil, munching on silicon chips, and watching "Brady Bunch" reruns.

Stay tuned . . .

ABOUT THE AUTHOR

Bill Myers is the author and co-creator of the best-selling "McGee and Me!" book and video series, which has sold 1.8 million episodes and has appeared several times as ABC's Weekend Special. He has written more than three dozen books and his work as a film maker has earned over 40 national and international awards. When he's not roaming the world making movies, he enjoys speaking at conferences and working with the youth of his local church. Bill lives in California with his wife, Brenda, and their two children.

You'll want to read them all.

THE INCREDIBLE WORLDS OF
WALLY McDOOGLE

#1—My Life As a Smashed Burrito with Extra Hot Sauce

Twelve-year-old Wally—"The walking disaster area"—is forced to stand up to Camp Wahkah Wahkah's number one all-American bad guy. One hilarious mishap follows another until, fighting together for their very lives, Wally learns the need for even his worst enemy to receive Jesus Christ. (ISBN 0–8499–3402–8)

#2—My Life As Alien Monster Bait

"Hollyweird" comes to Middletown! Wally's a superstar! A movie company has chosen our hero to be eaten by their mechanical "Mutant from Mars!" It's a close race as to which will consume Wally first—the disaster-plagued special effects "monster" or his own out-of-control pride . . . until he learns the cost of true friendship and of God's command for humility. (ISBN 0–8499–3403–6)

#3—My Life As a Broken Bungee Cord

A hot-air balloon race! What could be more fun? Then again, we're talking about Wally McDoogle, the "Human Catastrophe." Calamity builds on calamity until, with his life on the line, Wally learns what it means to FULLY put his trust in God. (ISBN 0–8499–3404–4)

#4—My Life As Crocodile Junk Food

Wally visits missionary friends in the South American rain forest. Here he stumbles onto a whole new set of impossible predicaments . . . until he understands the need and joy of sharing Jesus Christ with others. (ISBN 0–8499–3405–2)

#5—My Life As Dinosaur Dental Floss

It starts with a practical joke that snowballs into near disaster. Risking his life to protect his country, Wally is pursued by a SWAT team, bungling terrorists, photo-snapping tourists, Gary the Gorilla, and a TV news reporter. After prehistoric-size mishaps and a talk with the President, Wally learns that maybe honesty really is the best policy.
(ISBN 0–8499–3537–7)

#6—My Life As a Torpedo Test Target

Wally uncovers the mysterious secrets of a sunken submarine. As dreams of fame and glory increase, so do the famous McDoogle mishaps. Besides hostile sea creatures, hostile pirates, and hostile Wally McDoogle clumsiness, there is the war against his own greed and selfishness. It isn't until Wally finds himself on a wild ride atop a misguided torpedo that he realizes the source of true greatness.
(ISBN 0–8499–3538–5)

#7—My Life As a Human Hockey Puck

Look out . . . Wally McDoogle turns athlete! Jealousy and envy drive Wally from one hilarious calamity to another until, as the team's mascot, he learns humility while suddenly being thrown in to play goalie for the Middletown Super Chickens! (ISBN 0–8499–3601–2)

#8—My Life As an Afterthought Astronaut

"Just 'cause I didn't follow the rules doesn't make it my fault that the Space Shuttle almost crashed. Well, okay, maybe it was sort of my fault. But not the part when Pilot O'Brien was spacewalking and I accidently knocked him halfway to Jupiter. . . ." So begins another hilarious Wally McDoogle MISadventure as our boy blunder stows aboard the Space Shuttle and learns the importance of: Obeying the Rules! (ISBN 0–8499–3602–0)

#9—My Life As Reindeer Road Kill

Santa on an out-of-control four wheeler? Electrical Rudolph on the rampage? Nothing unusual, just Wally McDoogle doing some last-minute Christmas shopping . . . FOR GOD! Our boy blunder dreams that an angel has invited him to a birthday party for Jesus. Chaos and comedy follow as he turns the town upside down looking for the perfect gift, until he finally bumbles his way into the real reason for the Season. (ISBN 0–8499–3866–x)

#10—My Life As a Toasted Time Traveler

Wally travels back from the future to warn himself of an upcoming accident. But before he knows it, there are more Wallys running around than even Wally himself can handle. Catastrophes reach an all-time high as Wally tries to out-think God and re-write history. (ISBN 0–8499–3867–8)

Look for this humorous fiction series
at your local Christian bookstore.